FIC Rose
Rose, Elisabeth, 1951-
The right chord

THE RIGHT CHORD

THE RIGHT CHORD

•

Elisabeth Rose

AVALON BOOKS
NEW YORK

© Copyright 2007 by Elisabeth Hoorweg
All rights reserved.
All the characters in this book are fictitious,
and any resemblance to actual persons,
living or dead, is purely coincidental.
Published by Thomas Bouregy & Co., Inc.
160 Madison Avenue, New York, NY 10016

Library of Congress Cataloging-in-Publication Data

Rose, Elisabeth, 1951–
The right chord / Elisabeth Rose.
p. cm.
ISBN 978-0-8034-9824-2 (hardcover : acid-free paper)
1. Women musicians—Fiction. I. Title.

PR9619.4.R64R54 2007
813'.6—dc22

2006101707

PRINTED IN THE UNITED STATES OF AMERICA
ON ACID-FREE PAPER
BY HADDON CRAFTSMEN, BLOOMSBURG, PENNSYLVANIA

To Colin, Carla and Nick.

Denali who lives next door—the real Woof.

Chapter One

"It's hopeless having an argument with you," shouted Jeremy furiously just before he slammed out of the house. "You always see the other person's point of view."

"I thought that might have been a good thing," murmured Grace in surprise as the door crashed into its frame and the echo and his words resounded in her head. She stood blankly in the hallway for a few moments wondering what this particular, one-sided fight had been about. She often lost track. Jeremy seemed to be able to whip himself into a fury over the smallest things, and now she herself was the problem because she couldn't argue properly.

Grace opened the door tentatively, still quivering from the shock and the violence of his rage. Jeremy was striding down the footpath towards his lowslung sporty something or other. She could never remember the make of cars. It was dark blue that's about the best she could do. Midnight blue, he insisted.

"Jeremy," she called and ran down the three front steps and along the red brick path to the little lopsided, wrought iron gate which never closed because its hinges were rusted. He stopped, took one look and hissed with more venom than she'd ever heard from him, "For goodness sake! Go back inside! You're not . . ." His automatic car opener chirped as he pressed the button furiously.

A tall man with a large, gray and white dog at his heels paused and stared curiously as she stood being abandoned and chastised in full public view on a Tuesday morning. The dog sat down plumply and grinned at her with his red tongue lolling out. His tail swished on the path.

Grace experienced enlightenment of the worst kind. She hadn't finished dressing properly. Hadn't really started because Jeremy had turned up unexpectedly to retrieve some books he'd loaned her and caught her still in bed. Her exotic, pink, Chinese robe with the elaborate dragon embroidered on it only came to mid-thigh on a tiny Chinese girl and Grace was neither tiny nor Chinese. She'd bought it because she fell in love with the dragon. Unbrushed, wayward brown curls fell in her eyes—no make-up, bare feet with plum colored nails, bare legs, silver ankle bracelet. Grace smiled with as much dignity as she could manage.

"I think you look lovely," the stranger said quietly looking her straight in the eye. Grace gasped and backed towards the house.

The stranger gave her the impression he was about to say something else but decided against it and they walked on. The dog sniffed interestedly at the sporty something's tire and she prayed he'd pee on it. He lifted his leg.

"Get that animal away from there," she heard Jeremy snap before she closed the door hurriedly.

Grace trailed back to the kitchen and slumped down at the table. Eric was there slurping cereal and reading the paper in boxer shorts and a T-shirt. Another thing Jeremy detested, people lounging around in their night attire in the mornings instead of dressing properly. Especially at this hour, nine fifteen—mid-morning he called it but he hadn't had a concert to play at last night.

Eric glanced up. A drop of milk ran down his chin over the stubble.

"What was that about?" He caught the drop with the back of his hand.

"Apparently I don't know how to argue properly."

"You don't."

"Don't I?" Grace asked in surprise. "Does it annoy you?"

"No. I don't like fights."

"Neither do I," said Grace.

"We're too agreeable," said Eric and spooned cereal into his mouth.

"Jeremy's very angry."

"He always seems to be angry. He'll get ulcers. Is he coming back?"

Grace's eyes filled with tears. "I don't know." She sniffed and wiped her eyes quickly before Eric noticed. Although that was doubtful at the best of times.

"Hope not," said Eric. He stood up and took his bowl to the sink where he filled it with water and left it. Another thing which infuriated Jeremy. Grace wasn't keen on the practice either but let it go in the interests of peace and harmony. Jeremy had no such flexibility.

"Either stack it to be washed or wash the thing properly," he'd say in a tense, ulcer cultivating voice as he surveyed the kitchen from behind his immaculate, three piece suit. "I hate dishes piled in the sink filled with water. It's so tacky."

"He's changed," said Grace apologetically. She knew Eric put up with Jeremy for her sake alone. Eric had been her friend for a long time. Since grade school. "I thought he was different when we started dating. He was thoughtful and witty and charming."

"And now he's an anally retentive pain in the butt," said Eric succinctly. "Typical lawyer." He leaned against the bench with his arms folded. His boxer shorts had little musical instruments dancing all over them. A birthday present from Grace.

"That's not really fair," said Grace. "I've met some of his lawyer friends and they were very nice."

"Having one of them in the house is a different matter altogether," said Eric, as if he'd roomed with countless, insufferably difficult lawyers in his time. Which he hadn't. He'd roomed with Grace and another violinist before their current housemate, bass player Marcel, moved in. "Pedantry is not an endearing quality."

"True." Grace sighed. "We'd better get ready."

"His problem is," said Eric as they went to dress and shower respectively, "he doesn't understand the artistic nature. He thinks we're slackers and that being a musician isn't a real job."

"He used to think it made me interesting and exotic that I played violin. Now he's annoyed because I'm out at night and sleep in in the mornings."

"While he's off defending criminals," said Eric going into his bedroom. "And letting them loose on society."

"Apparently he's very good at it," replied Grace. She had the distinct feeling she wouldn't see Jeremy again. That slamming door had the ring of finality. And the fact he'd come unannounced to collect his possessions in the first place implied a closing down and moving on.

Why had Jeremy become involved with her and this chaotic household inhabited by three musicians and the neighbour's cat? Grace brushed her hair and applied make-up as she pondered the question. They were physically attracted to each other, that was beyond doubt, he also liked her calmness, he said. He found her soothing and he liked the way she dressed in bright colors and loose flowing skirts and blouses with plunging necklines. The women he normally associated with wore suits of gray or black and were wound tight as watch springs. Brittle and hard. He liked that Grace was soft and sexy, feminine and gentle.

Now she was too conciliatory and casual and sloppy and her friends were worse. The alliance was doomed from the start she realized now. He'd been trying something different, like a new coat or a car and she hadn't fitted, didn't suit his lifestyle he realized after a test drive.

Grace peered at her reflection. Was *she* the problem? Should she make changes? Was the world—meaning men—passing her by because she was impossible to put up with? Too vague, too easy-going?

Jeremy became infuriated because she wouldn't take a stance on some issue that she found extremely uninteresting. Usually political and usually connected with vast amounts of money and the wielding of power. She supposed they mattered to someone. Jeremy certainly took these things personally. He was very ambitious and wanted her to be, too. Maybe she should become harder and more driven. Less accepting, more demanding. It sounded very tiring.

She was an artist, a musician and preferred to lose herself in swirling harmonies and pulsating rhythms. Grace liked to entertain people and take them away from themselves in music rather than add to the tensions and worries of the world.

The roaring of a truck's engine made her peer out her bedroom window. A green furniture van had pulled up next door blocking most of the street. That man with the soothing voice and his lovely dog were standing watching as two men jumped out and opened the big back door to their truck.

She'd call Jeremy this afternoon and see if she could pacify him and patch things up.

"Are you ready?" called Eric through the half closed door.

Grace sat miserably in the fourth desk first violins next to Edward who was middle-aged and gray and wore brocade waistcoats over black shirts and had a wife who painted delicate watercolors of flowers and fruit. She doubted Jeremy would call. He always left it to her to make the first conciliatory gesture. She could call to say she'd found a tie he'd taken off one night and left in the living room after dinner. It had disappeared beneath the sofa cushions. Marcel found it and borrowed it to wear to a gig.

Efficiency was Jeremy's middle name, the forgotten tie was an aberration which he was sure to correct. In no time, all traces of Jeremy could be removed from Curston Road. In the twinkle of an eye. Or the fall of a teardrop.

The conductor arrived at the podium and Grace roused herself to play Tschaikovsky whose swirling, yearning, passionate music suited her dismal mood perfectly. In the break, as they ate biscuits and drank tea, Edward muttered dire things to her about Patsy who sat in front of them, third desk violins. Edward resented the players in the front desks and thought he should be at least second desk. They all played the same music for heaven's sake, what was the big deal?

"I don't know how she got that position," he hissed to Grace for the millionth time. "Her bowing is all over the place, and if she mentions to me just once more how she played under Andre Previn in London I'll wrap her bow around her neck."

Patsy irritated Grace too, in a mild sort of way but until now she had nodded and made noncommittal murmurings whenever Edward embarked on one of his diatribes. Time to be more decisive she suddenly decided. She was sick of Edward going on and on and never shutting up about his problems and his ambitions and his frustrations. He hadn't even noticed she was glum and teary eyed. It wouldn't occur to him to ask was she feeling all right. Was she ill? Had someone died? Had her heart been broken?

"Patsy can be a bit of a pain sometimes," she said clearly and Edward looked at her in amazement. "Everyone is a pain sometimes, Edward, even you and probably me, but can't we talk about something else? Instead of complaining all the time?"

Grace held her breath after this outburst and knew her face was bright red. She had never within living memory raised her voice or made her feelings so blatantly obvious.

"I'm sorry, Grace," Edward stuttered.

Far from being angry as she expected, Grace saw that

he was so startled his brain had ceased to function or at least, to connect with his mouth. His face was bright red too and his little, thin-lipped mouth flapped open and closed. He looked like a grouper, that big ugly fish. Grace giggled nervously and said in a shaky voice, "I'm sorry Edward. I'm a bit—emotional today. I've . . ."

Edward's face relaxed into a condescending expression of great understanding. He leaned forward and patted Grace's arm. He lowered his voice confidentially.

"That's okay, Grace. I know, girl's problems. Between you and me, Felice turns into an absolute dragon every month."

It was Grace's turn to gape. Should she put him straight? The old Grace resurfaced. Why bother? From long experience she knew it wouldn't matter what she said, Edward would happily think what he liked and if she told him she was about to be dumped he'd be even more embarrassingly conciliatory. She produced a feeble smile.

"Poor Felice," she said and Edward nodded sagely.

"Yes. I can tell you it takes every ounce of my patience sometimes."

"She's lucky you're so understanding."

Edward patted her arm again. "Let me get you another cup of tea, Grace."

When Grace got home that afternoon the furniture movers were going full steam strolling in and out and yelling laconic instructions to each other. The house had had a FOR SALE sign on it for weeks and then the agent plastered a red SOLD sticker diagonally across it. Grace watched a couple of men in green T-shirts and shorts unloading a beautiful, old, wing backed armchair from the gigantic green van and wondered who would be the new neighbor. Someone who didn't mind music she hoped. Mary and Felix on the other side were out all day at work, which was why Brandy the cat came to visit, and chances are these people would be the same.

Marcel had left a scrawled note on the kitchen table for Grace, saying, '*That uptight guy came and took his tie. I didn't let him into your room in case he stole something.*'

Grace's eyes filled with tears but she smiled at the same time. Marcel was like a big, protective, guard dog. She suspected Jeremy was slightly afraid of him. Marcel was well over six feet tall, had a beard and longish hair tied back in a pony tail, and tattoos. He had roared at Jeremy one evening when Jeremy had moved his double bass.

"Nobody touches my bass!" he thundered and Grace could see Jeremy weighing up the possible outcomes of the ensuing damages action after Marcel had torn both his arms off.

"The man's crazy," he'd muttered to Grace indignantly and she soothed and stroked and explained how Marcel's bass was extremely valuable as were all their instruments and no musician liked a stranger touching their tools of trade. Apparently neither of her roommates had liked her choice of boyfriend but had been too polite to tell her. She was, typically, the last to know.

She got out her violin to practise Tschaikovsky and then moved on to their other piece which was awkward and modern and most of the orchestra hated with a passion. Eric was in his room practising it already on his trombone. She could hear all sorts of flatulent noises coming down the hallway.

Grace packed away her violin at about four. She dialled Jeremy's number at work and was put, surprisingly, straight through to him.

"Hello," she said nervously to his brusque hello.

"I'm glad you called," he said as if she were a client with a problem whose solution he had found. He didn't wait to hear why she'd called, he assumed he knew. "I think it's time we called it a day, Grace. Things just aren't working out, are they?"

"Do you think so?" she cried and her carefully prepared apology shattered. "Can't we talk about it, at least?"

"There's no point, Grace," he answered briskly. "I'm not the right man for you." That was his tactful way of saying she was all wrong for him. "A clean break is best, I think."

What could she say? Begging and tearful pleading was next on the list but she didn't want to make it more excruciating for either of them. She was hopeless at break-ups. Jeremy was an expert she now discovered as he made a businesslike farewell and disconnected. Grace found herself listening to the dialtone even as she said goodbye.

A part of her admired his technique. She couldn't extract herself from a relationship as surgically as that. In the past, several men had dated her for weeks after she'd grown tired of them purely because she was too kind-hearted to tell them what Jeremy had just told her. Eventually they had drifted away of their own accord and Grace had heaved a sigh of relief.

But Jeremy was different. She wasn't tired of Jeremy. He could be difficult and sometimes pedantic but she enjoyed going out with him. He had impeccable manners and liked doing things in style, taking note of her likes and dislikes, listening to her opinions even if he didn't agree. He made her feel special—his Princess Grace. She enjoyed the parties they went to, and the people she met there all seemed to like her. He had a very wide ranging social circle in the very upscale set. She thought they, and Jeremy, enjoyed her eclectic, arty style of dress and the fact that she was non-competitive in his very competitive world. She thought he liked to show her off.

And she liked his kisses and the way he caught her with that little, private, half smile that made her smile and look away in case she laughed when they were at some otherwise stuffy event.

Grace went sadly to the kitchen and began to prepare a casserole. She liked to cook, and the men liked to eat.

The only dish Marcel could make was curry so his cooking nights were necessarily limited by the others to once a week. Eric could manage spaghetti bolognese and do a mean barbecue in the summer.

Marcel came in soon after with Kirsty. He'd met her at a jazz festival where she was singing with a blues band. Now they worked together in the same group. Grace liked Kirsty. She had the strength and forcefulness Grace wished for herself.

"Did you see my note?" asked Marcel as he flung open the fridge and grabbed the jug of his homemade juice. Jungle Juice he called it. Grace already had a consoling glass going while she chopped and peeled. Not a bad brew this time—apple, cucumber and carrot. Some of his supposedly healthy concoctions were hideous.

"Yes." Grace kept her head lowered because she knew she'd cry in front of them if she met anyone's eye. She'd managed to keep Jeremy out of her thoughts while she practiced, before the final phone call, but now his face kept creeping back in. The way his blue eyes lit up when he laughed and that confident air he had of always being right. She liked that, and the way he dressed, and the way he kissed her.

"What?" asked Kirsty suspiciously, looking from one to the other and pausing on Grace. Grace could feel her brown eyes boring into the back of her head as she dumped chopped onions into a hot pan.

"Jeremy's gone," said Grace when it became obvious Marcel wasn't going to say anything.

"Oh, Grace," said Kirsty and jumped up to put her arms around her from behind. That did it. Tears flowed in copious quantities as Grace was enveloped in Kirsty's perfume and her motherly embrace. She turned and sobbed into Kirsty's red crushed velvet clad shoulder.

"Good riddance," remarked Marcel calmly.

"Shut up," said Kirsty. "Take no notice of that big dope, Grace." She patted Grace's back firmly like a mother burping a baby. "Jeremy was a bit of a shocker, though. Those ties he wore—baby puke yellow."

"That one he left here was all right. Except it's got tomato sauce on it now," said Marcel.

Grace giggled through the flood and pulled away from Kirsty who gave her a comforting squeeze and let her go. Kirsty picked up the wooden spoon and gave the browning onions a stir while Grace fled to the bathroom to splash water on her eyes and make sure her mascara wasn't all over her face like a racoon.

When she returned Marcel was on his second glass of Jungle Juice and Kirsty had begun browning the meat. The smell was delicious.

"Staying for dinner, Kirsty?" asked Grace.

"Yes please," she replied promptly. "Tell me what happened?"

"I wasn't the sort of girl he wanted. He said I'm too casual and sloppy and I don't know how to argue properly. I'm too easy-going. He said we should call it a day."

"What an expression! But did you want to break up?" asked Kirsty.

"No," said Grace and it was true. "I thought we could work things out. He seemed to get upset very easily. But I can change."

"Why should you do that?" interrupted Marcel. "Especially for a no-hoper like him."

"It's not just Jeremy," said Grace slowly. "I think he's right. I am too easy-going. I let people take advantage of me. In lots of little things. People push me out of the way in lines, I'm always last to be served at the stores and I never complain or take things back when they're wrong or don't work. I always listen to people going on and on about their problems when they're not the slightest bit interested in mine. Edward does it to me all the time. Until today. I told him he should talk about something other than himself and stop constantly complaining about Patsy and he was amazed. It felt pretty good, actually."

"Has it ever bothered you before?" asked Kirsty.

Grace shook her head. "I always feel if it's that important to them to be first on the bus . . ." She shrugged. "Let them. We all get there at the same time."

Eric came in and sat down next to Marcel. "What are we talking about?" he asked.

"Grace has decided she's too easy going," said Kirsty.

"But that's why we love her," said Eric lightly.

"It's that rotten Jeremy's fault," said Marcel and thumped his hand on the table. "I never trusted that guy."

"That's only because he touched your bass," said Grace indignantly. Something fired inside her. "And you do leave it in the living room where we all have to walk around it. It gets in the way, Marcel and one day someone will fall over it and damage it."

"Way to go, Grace!" cried Kirsty, grinning from ear to ear at the shocked expression on her boyfriend's face.

"I'm sorry you feel that way," said Marcel stiffly. "I had no idea."

"No, I know," said Grace, her face hot. "You all just assume I won't mind. And it was my fault for letting you. I've been too weak. Things are going to be different now."

Eric and Marcel eyed each other uneasily. Grace turned her back on them and poured a generous amount of red wine into the sizzling meat and onions. She added herbs, a stock cube, water, the other vegetables and a grind of pepper and shoved it into the oven. Kirsty helped clear away the debris of vegetable peels and wiped down the counter.

"Come and sit in the garden," Grace said. They left the two men muttering together in a worried undertone and went out the back door to the spacious yard.

In between playing his bass and sleeping, Marcel loved pottering in the garden and he had a tidy little vegetable patch flourishing in one corner. He wasn't keen on flowers but Grace had cajoled him into planting a few along the fence on the side of the new neighbor. The grass was reasonably under control too, thanks to his ministrations with the mower borrowed from across the street.

They sat on two rickety, wooden garden chairs in the last of the afternoon sunshine.

"So! The new Grace rises from the ashes of the Jeremy fiasco," said Kirsty dramatically.

"I have to do something." said Grace seriously. She twirled her glass in her hand. "I mean it."

"Why?" asked Kirsty quietly. "You're a lovely person, Grace. You're one of the kindest people I know."

"Look at me Kirsty. I'm nearly thirty one. I've had more boyfriends than I can remember and none of them lasted more than six months. They're attracted to me initially and then they get bored because I'm not a very interesting person. I have to make myself more interesting. Kind? Doormat more like it."

"What are you going to do? Take up skydiving or something? Learn Chinese? Memorize the whole of Shakespeare's poetry? Become a Star Wars fanatic? They'd find that interesting." Kirsty gave a shout of laughter.

Grace looked up quickly. "I hadn't thought of that. Maybe I will." She laughed at the look on Kirsty's round, friendly face. "Not watch Star Wars movies, learn something. Italian. I might try Italian. I know some already. *Presto, allegro con brio, forte*," she declaimed with rolling r's and extravagant gestures.

"Can't hurt."

"And I'm going to change my attitude. No more Ms Nice Girl."

"To do it right you're going to have to dress differently," said Kirsty sitting forward eagerly. "Tight skirts, gray, black, brown, tailored slacks. Cream, blue, pastel gray blouses and jackets. You're nice and slim. It'd suit you. I'd look like an overstuffed sausage." She paused, studying Grace who sat in her white, lace blouse and red-patterned, ankle length skirt. "Power dressing. You know what they look like, you see them in the city. All business suits and briefcases and faces carved from granite. And maybe cut your hair."

Grace's hand flew to her thick shoulder length tresses and she spilled Jungle Juice on the grass. She put the glass down carefully.

"Do you think so?" she asked doubtfully.

"Either that or wear it in a bun. Up somehow anyway. Riotous curls are gorgeous but very unbusinesslike, Grace."

"I think I'll wear it up," said Grace. "I don't think I could bear to cut it."

Kirsty nodded. "Want me to come shopping?"

Grace bit her lip. This half baked idea of hers was snowballing and threatening to run out of control. But something had to change, she had to take action because no-one else would do it for her. In a funny sort of way she could thank Jeremy for dumping her and giving her this wake up call. But it was humiliating and it hurt because she really thought she loved Jeremy despite his faults. He hadn't even called her to make up or break up. Hadn't left a note with Marcel when he collected his tie. Nothing. He'd expected her to make the first move and she had. Grace had an unaccustomed flicker of an emotion she'd never experienced before.

"What would be really satisfying," she said. "Is to turn into the sort of person Jeremy wants and win him back and then dump him."

"Now you're getting the idea!" said Kirsty with great satisfaction.

"Power dressing," mused Grace. Maybe if she got the outer shell right the inner core would toughen up as well. No more scouring market stalls and ethnic clothing shops for exotic little bits and pieces to fling together in her eclectic wardrobe. Designer labels from now on, sleek and sophisticated. "I'll make up a schedule for cooking and cleaning too. I seem to cook more than any one else and if I didn't clean the bathroom no-one would."

"Really?!" exclaimed Kirsty. "How could you let them get away with that, Grace? That's positively stone age."

"Eric vacuums and takes out the garbage," said Grace, "and Marcel takes care of the garden. It's not as bad as it sounds."

"Wrong, Grace. You've slipped back. You can't think like that. That's the old Grace talking not the new woman," said Kirsty sternly.

"Ooh. I don't think I'm going to be very good at this."

"Yes, you are. You just have to say to yourself 'Do I honestly mind doing this?' or 'Do I mind that person pushing me out of the way?' If the answer is yes, fight back. Stand up for your rights. 'I am woman hear me roar'," she sang loudly.

"Okay. I'll try. I'll be more aggressive and I won't let people push me around."

"Operation Revenge on Jeremy is under way," cried Kirsty and raised her glass. Grace found herself smiling in anticipation at the look on his face when she appeared casually before him in her new persona. Cool, sophisticated, tough, desirable and unattainable.

She raised her glass and clinked it with Kirsty's but her free hand ran up and down the soft, pliable, cotton fabric of her favourite Fijian, wrap-around skirt.

Chapter Two

Next door, Harry Birmingham flopped thankfully into his favorite armchair. The one he'd found in the secondhand furniture store. So what if it had a small stain on one arm and was a little threadbare in places? It was an old-fashioned, wing backed chair exactly like the one his grandfather had had. Exactly the sort of thing Janis detested. They were hard to find nowadays especially in this original, dark red, velvety fabric.

Harry stuck his feet up on the coffee table and vowed he'd never move house again. Woof stuck his cold, wet nose into Harry's hand as it dangled down by the side of the chair. He patted the gray, furry head.

"That's it, Woof. We've finished. Like it here?"

Woof didn't answer. He wandered away and lay down in front of the empty fireplace. Harry watched him pensively. He should do something about dinner. He didn't have the energy. Take-away, the ideal solution. He rang the Thai restaurant whose flier he'd discovered in the pile of junk mail in his new mailbox.

Living alone was going to take some getting used to. He was basically a home loving family man, always had been and now that family had disintegrated into separate entities. Him here with the dog in Sydney suburbia Curston Road and Janis with her upward career path in her unit in upmarket, harborside Birchgrove. Eight year old William, the most important and treasured of all the entities floated between the two. Harry supposedly saw him weekends and holidays but Janis's busy and highly motivated life meant William spent far more time than that with Harry. Which suited Harry just fine. Four more days before William came to sleep in the room he had chosen as his when they were making the decision about this house.

His dinner arrived in plastic containers. Harry ate it in his new kitchen with Woof sitting anxiously at his feet with an expectant look on his face. Harry ignored him and threw the remains in the garbage. He said, "Come on. Walk." Woof leapt up with an excited bark and they went to explore the neighbourhood.

The house on one side seemed to be occupied by a middle aged working couple with teenage sons and the other by at least one musician. Harry speculated as to whether the trombone he'd heard was played by the obnoxious turnip who'd snapped at Woof this morning.

And whether that pretty woman in the pink wrap was his unfortunate wife, standing in the garden with such a heartbroken expression. He wondered if she'd been offended by his comment and whether he'd have the jerk at his door complaining about how Harry had upset his wife. She had a gorgeous smile.

Now, as he and Woof returned from their walk a large, hairy man came out carrying a double bass. He reminded Harry immediately of a yeti. A woman with tousled red hair, a silver nose stud and tight black pants held the door open for him. She wasn't nearly as attractive as the other one but had a friendly face.

Harry paused as the man blocked the path with his bass, and said, "Hello, I've just moved in next door."

The woman came towards them grinning and said in a surprisingly deep and melodious voice, "Hello. I'm Kirsty. I don't live here. Marcel does. What a fabulous dog."

She bent down and started rubbing Woof's head between both her hands and exclaiming over his looks. He wagged his tail furiously and tried to lick her. The bass player propped his instrument against the battered station wagon in the gutter and stuck out his hand.

"Marcel Fraillon," he said.

"Harry Birmingham."

"The writer?" Startling blue eyes twinkled out of the undergrowth and white teeth flashed in a smile. Harry nodded.

"Cool! I've read all your stuff, man." Marcel pumped

his hand with renewed vigor. Kirsty had straightened up and was regarding him with interest.

Harry, embarrassed as always by recognition, said, "Thank-you. I sometimes wonder if anyone reads what I write."

"Of course they do," exclaimed Kirsty. "*Shadow Music* is my all time favorite."

"Come over and visit some time. Meet the others," said Marcel. "I'm on my way to a gig, now. Sorry, running late. Honor to meet you, Harry." He carefully loaded the bass into the car. Kirsty blew Harry a kiss as they drove away.

The next day Grace came home from rehearsal to find Eric and Marcel comfortably ensconced in the kitchen with an unknown man and three glasses of Marcel's, this time vile, mustard colored, Jungle Juice. They were laughing uproariously over some outrageous story Marcel was telling and, as Grace entered, a big gray and white dog came out from under the table to sniff at her legs suspiciously. Both visitors looked disturbingly familiar and she suddenly, with a prickle of discomfort, remembered the man who had witnessed Jeremy's departure and been the subject of his wrath. And his remark.

The dog's tail began to wag slowly but Grace resisted the temptation to kneel down and hug him and introduce herself. Instead, she gave him a quick pat on the head before deciding the new Grace didn't want a strange dog in the kitchen. She'd never been keen on animals in the house. Small ones, maybe, but this one was huge, some sort of husky perhaps. He'd leave hairs everywhere and doggy smells. The old Grace would have let it go, not wanting to upset the owner but the new Grace drew a deep breath and said, "Hello everyone."

Eric said, "Harry, this is Grace. Grace, this is Harry. From next door. And that's Woof."

"Hello, Harry." Grace smiled and took the plunge keeping her face averted from Woof whose brown eyes gazed up at her adoringly. "Would you mind if Woof went outside? I really prefer not to have animals in the kitchen. Hygiene and all that . . ." Her burst of temerity fizzled and she caught the surprised faces of her roommates from the corner of her eye.

"I'm sorry."

The man uncurled himself from the chair and flicked his fingers at the dog who immediately darted to his side. He opened the door and told Woof to 'Stay' on the back step. Grace caught a glimpse of the dog as he flopped down untidily and rested his head on his front paws. She had an irrational urge to tell him he wasn't in trouble because he looked so forlorn. He really was a beautiful animal.

Harry came back inside and held out his hand. He had gray eyes which ran up and down her body quickly, assessing her and apparently dismissing her because they didn't linger for very long at all. Grace looked up into his face as she shook his hand and was immediately thrown off balance. He had a *very* interesting face. She liked the way lines appeared at the sides of his mouth when he smiled and the way his longish, light brown hair was brushed away from his wide forehead and curled over the collar of his casual cotton shirt.

"How do you do?" His voice was warm and gentle. "Harry Birmingham."

"Grace Richmond."

"You play in the orchestra with Eric?" Harry asked and indicated his chair. She smiled but shook her head at the offer and he sat back down.

"Yes."

Grace opened the fridge and got out the bottle of mineral water. There was no evidence of any dinner under way. She glanced at her watch. It was Eric's turn to cook. Normally she would have unquestioningly begun to prepare something but not tonight. He'd had the afternoon off, he had no excuse, the schedule was quite clear. They'd eaten Marcel's curry last night to prove it.

She sat at the table and gave her skirt a little tug to cover her thighs. Her new clothes felt stiff and strange and each time she caught sight of her reflection it startled her so that she looked over her shoulder to see who the stern woman was behind her. Today she was wearing a slimfitting gray skirt and tight, sleeveless, black top. Her hair was piled up and held with a tortoise shell clasp and was the one failure in her no nonsense appearance. No matter how hard she tried she couldn't prevent curly tendrils escaping and hanging around her neck and cheeks.

Sitting down was a major drawback to wearing these skirts, she'd discovered. She'd have to wear trousers to rehearsals in future because most of the session had been spent trying to avoid indecent exposure. Plus Edward had positively leered at her legs.

"When's your next concert?" asked Harry. He glanced at her legs too then away again.

"Saturday," said Eric. "Like to stay for dinner, Harry? Okay, Grace?"

"Sure," said Grace, hoping no-one noticed her excessively hot cheeks. "It's your turn to cook."

"Is it? I'd completely forgotten." Eric laughed and looked at her expectantly. Grace took a sip of water.

"What do you do, Harry?" she asked, ignoring Eric completely.

"I'm a writer," he said. "And I lecture at Sydney University."

"How interesting," she replied, surprised and somehow pleased that he should be an artist too. "Fiction writer?"

"Yes."

"He writes Science Fiction," said Marcel. "Haven't you heard of him?"

"Oh. No," she said and felt Harry's curious gaze upon her. "Sorry."

Grace drank more water. She always found sci fi impenetrable and pointless, preferring historicals, romances and detective stories. The old Grace wouldn't have said so but neither would the new Grace. She wanted to be assertive not offensive.

Harry drained his glass and stood up. "I won't stay to eat thanks, Eric," he said.

"Why not?" asked Marcel. "Grace can whip us up something. She's an expert cook."

"No, she can't," replied Grace, smiling pleasantly. "It's Eric's turn." Harry gave her a studied look. "We have a schedule," she explained.

"We can send out for takeout," said Eric hastily. "But you're better off coming back on Grace's cooking night."

"No thanks, I'd better take Woof out for a walk," said Harry. "It was very nice to meet you, Eric. Thanks for the drink. Good night, Grace."

Marcel got up to show him out and came back with a frown.

"That was a bit rude, Grace," he said, sounding puzzled and hurt.

"What?" she asked and Eric chimed in, "Kicking his dog out. And you know you could have whipped something up for dinner."

"Why should I?" she retorted.

"I don't know. To be friendly."

"This is the new Grace, Eric, remember," said Marcel.

"I like our old one better," grumbled Eric.

"That's because she didn't complain and she let you two take advantage of her. It's the principle of the thing." Grace raised her glass to Marcel who clinked his against it. "What's for dinner, Eric? I'm hungry."

"Me too." Marcel poured himself more juice.

"Pizza."

"On the other hand, maybe this will completely backfire," said Grace as Eric went to phone the pizza shop. "Pizza every third night alternating with curry could be a problem. You'll have to expand your repertoires." She grinned at Marcel. "I quite like the new me."

"I don't think Harry did much," said Marcel.

"Too bad," said Grace but part of her was a little bit sorry because their new neighbor held a certain indefinable attraction and it wasn't just his lovely big dog.

The lovely big dog paid them a visit the next day. He pushed his head through a gap in the derelict paling fence, squeezed his body after, squashed some agapanthus and dahlias and ran around the lawn with his nose on the ground. Grace was in the kitchen making coffee and saw him trespassing. Brandy, the ginger cat from the other side was sunning herself on the garden path, her favorite spot, sunwarmed red bricks to snooze and stretch upon.

Woof spied her within seconds and it was on for young and old. Brandy streaked across the grass and up into the nearest high refuge which happened to be a birch tree next to Marcel's vegetable patch. Big paws scattered lettuces, trampled carrots and knocked down carefully staked tomatoes.

Grace rushed outside, yelling at the invader. He turned, gave her a sheepish look and to her surprise stopped what he was doing and came meekly to her side with his tail wagging ingratiatingly.

"Bad boy!" she scolded. He dropped his head penitently. "Look at Marcel's garden. You're going to be in big trouble."

Woof licked her hand. Grace smiled down into his brown, doggy eyes. He was irresistible. She patted his head and then rubbed both hands down the length of his furry body. He tried to lick her face and she straightened, hooked her fingers into his collar and took him beside the house, along the footpath and into his own front yard. He followed obediently as she marched up the path to his front door. Time to be assertive. She rapped sharply and waited.

She heard footsteps coming along the hallway then Harry fiddling with the lock. The door swung open. Woof darted inside nearly ripping her fingers from her hand. Harry looked at her in bewilderment, then at Woof who had returned to sit beside him politely.

"Hello." He smiled. Grace's mind immediately went blank. The way his mouth creased at the corners wiped every thought from her head. "Where did you find Woof? I thought he was out the back."

Her brain jolted into gear. Focus. Be assertive. "Your

dog has just been rampaging around in our garden," said Grace sternly. "He's wrecked Marcel's vegetable patch chasing a cat. And squashed some dahlias." She stopped with her mouth clamped in a tight line waiting for the response. Had she overdone it? She had no idea how Harry would react.

"Did you do that?" Harry asked Woof and frowned. Woof looked up and panted happily. His tail went thump, thump on the polished, wooden floor. His muddy paws gave him away. Harry looked back at Grace and his face assumed a blank expression. "I'm sorry," he said. "I'll make sure he stays in, in the future."

"You'll need to fix the fence," she said stiffly through the surge of relief that he hadn't slammed the door in her face. "He pushed a loose paling off."

"All right," agreed Harry calmly. "Is that all?"

"Yes."

Grace turned away, uncomfortably conscious of his cool gaze, and walked back down the path to the small white gate. Roses grew all along the path and front fence and they were in full flower. The perfume was overpowering and Grace couldn't resist the urge to stop and bury her nose in one of the dark red blooms. Old Gordon who lived here previously used to give her big bunches of them. She would miss their chats over the fence and the odd cup of tea they shared. The new owner didn't seem the chatty type. More a beer with the guys kind of man.

She touched one of the velvety petals briefly with

her hand, remembering as she straightened up. Harry's voice called, "Pick some if you like." Grace hadn't realized he was still there on the step watching her.

"No, thanks all the same," she said, flustered—the new Grace doesn't stop nostalgically to smell the roses—and quickly marched along the footpath to her own house. She went out the back to survey the damage Woof had caused. It really wasn't bad. Mainly big paw prints in the soft earth. Brandy had come down from her perch and presumably gone home to recuperate from the shock.

Grace straightened up the bent dahlias and tomatoes and collected two lettuces which were knocked out of the ground. She smoothed out the earth around the carrots with a rake and optimistically stuck some of them back in the ground. As she pottered she could hear Harry hammering at the fence on his side.

She went inside to practise. They had a concert on Saturday and there were some bits she needed to work on.

Woof began to howl. The mournful wail rose and fell, gradually increasing in volume until she had to stop. It was such a dismal, ancient, wolflike, despairing sound Grace smiled and then giggled. What had set him off? Maybe the siren from an ambulance or a fire engine. The dog they'd had when she was a child had done that and they'd all thought it was funny to see little Trixie, the bitser, sitting with her nose in the air howling. Singing, her father said.

Marcel appeared, bleary eyed and dishevelled from sleep.

"What on earth's that?" he asked.

"It's Woof."

"Huh," grunted Marcel and disappeared into the kitchen. Grace started in on the piece again and within a few minutes Woof started to howl again.

"It's you," called Marcel from the kitchen. "He's joining in."

"What can I do?" asked Grace in frustration standing in the doorway, violin in one hand, bow in the other. "I have to be able to practice."

"Ignore him."

"How?"

Marcel shrugged. "It has a sort of cosmic flow to it, that sound. Primal. In touch with nature, tapping into our deepest being."

"He broke through the fence and chased Brandy through your vegetable patch," said Grace. She laughed. "That was very primal."

Marcel grabbed his cup of coffee and disappeared rapidly out the back door. Grace returned to the living room and tried again. She experimented with different volumes and sections and discovered that he preferred the modern piece with its swooping glissandi and high pitched trills.

"Hurts both our ears," she murmured sympathetically. But the problem remained. When she, and maybe

Eric, practised, Woof would howl and she doubted whether anybody would be able to stand the combination of both. And what about Harry? He was supposed to be a writer. He'd be on the doorstep next, complaining about the noise she was making.

He was. Twenty minutes later. Grace went to open the door. She'd seen him coming up the path and steeled herself. "Don't apologize," she said to herself fiercely. "You've nothing to be sorry for. Don't apologize!" She flung open the door.

"Hello," said Harry. "I suppose you know why I'm here?"

He didn't wait for an answer but held out a large bunch of roses. Grace stared at him in surprise.

"I'm really sorry about Woof," he said. "He's no music lover. Or maybe he is." He laughed and strands of the long, brown hair fell across his forehead. He ran his free hand through it to sweep it back.

"You mean he's criticizing my playing?" asked Grace desperately trying to stay focused and not be sidetracked by how alarmingly good-looking the man was and how Jeremy had never brought her flowers.

The smile left Harry's face. "No! Not at all," he said. "I mean, maybe that's his way of saying he likes it."

"He makes it difficult to practice," said Grace.

"And for me to work," said Harry in a different tone altogether.

"Are you telling me I shouldn't practice?" asked Grace. "I hope not."

"I came to offer my apologies and to give you these on Woof's behalf," said Harry without answering her question. "I don't want to start a war. I've only been here a few days."

Marcel came up the passage behind her. "Harry," he cried. "Come in. I'll give you a lettuce. Woof's already picked it for you."

Harry looked at Grace, the roses still extended towards her. She took them and stepped aside silently as he squeezed passed. He stopped halfway, his tall body with its surprisingly broad chest overwhelming her in the narrow space. She kept her head lowered and he said softly, "Can't we be friends?"

Grace felt her cheeks go pink. Why was she being prickly and difficult? It was unnatural. No-one had ever said that to her before because she *was* so very friendly. Indiscriminately so. That was her problem.

"Thanks for the roses." She gave him a cool glance before turning to go into the living room to find a vase in the sideboard. She heard Marcel offering Harry a cup of tea and when she went to fill the vase and arrange the beautiful roses at the kitchen counter they were sitting at the table as if they'd known each other for years.

"Cup of tea, Grace?" offered Marcel. Grace shook her head.

"No thanks, I've got more practice to do," she said and glanced at Harry then away quickly because he was staring at her so intently.

"Sorry about Woof," said Harry.

As Grace carried the flowers back to the living room she heard Marcel say, "Grace's not usually like that, Harry. She just got ditched by a real idiot of a guy so she's a bit touchy."

Grace quickly closed the living room door so she couldn't hear Harry's condescending reply. She knew what he'd say, he'd seen the idiot. Men! Who needs them?

At the concert Edward said, as they were waiting to go on stage, "Heard the news?"

"No, what news?" Grace always missed out on the gossip until Edward passed it on to her as he invariably did.

"Joan is leaving." He waited with an expectant expression for the effect of this bombshell to impact on Grace. He wasn't disappointed. She couldn't help the spontaneous cry of, "Why on earth is she going? She's been with us for ever."

"I know," agreed Edward. "She's been offered a teaching position and she wants to take it, apparently. Moving to Adelaide. Her son lives there with his family. Joan's getting older, you know."

"Adelaide?"

Edward nodded. "Her position is being advertised. I'm going to audition. Second desk, inside, right behind Stanislav." His satisfied expression indicated the audition process would be a mere formality.

"In front of Patsy," commented Grace drily. "When are the auditions?"

"In about six weeks."

"I might give it a try, too," she said, not really seriously.

"You?" he exclaimed and Edward's incredulous expression coupled with his response stung her to such a degree she made up her mind on the spot.

"Why not? I'm just as good a player as you, Edward." Better, New Grace thought but Old Grace never would have admitted.

Edward's mouth flapped like that big, old grouper again. "Yes, I know. I didn't mean—it's just that it's so unlike you, Grace. I thought you didn't care about desking."

"You'd better start practicing, Edward," she said serenely.

Eric's reaction when she told him at interval was much the same.

"Why bother?" he asked.

"Because Edward is," said Grace. "And this is the new me, remember? No more going with the flow. I have to be more decisive and progressive. Onward and upward."

"Do you?" said Eric and sighed.

At the next rehearsal Grace notified the manager of her intention to audition for Joan's position.

"We're expecting a lot of interest," he said. "I know of several very talented young players looking for an orchestral position with us."

"They can have my old seat," said Grace with determination and earned a very surprised look from Ian.

"Good luck," he said and added. "I've always thought you were better than fourth desk."

Grace glowed all the way home. And she began seriously to practice. One thing to learn the parts for their concert pieces, another to play a solo and outshine all the young turks flooding out of the Music Colleges, plus dazzle with knowledge of the repertoire and ability to sightread. There'd be contenders from overseas as well.

Woof joined in occasionally but Grace gritted her teeth and kept working. It'd be worse for Harry in the same house with him. He'd have to deal with it, not her.

Woof was sprawled on the footpath outside the supermarket when Grace swung around the corner armed with her shopping list for that night's dinner. She bent to pat him and he wagged his tail eagerly.

"That dog is blocking the entrance," said a cranky, female voice. "You should have more consideration."

Grace whipped around indignantly but the complainer had entered the shop and she was left standing open mouthed and redfaced. Inside, at the vegetable section, Harry held a mango up to his nose then put it back and squeezed another one. Grace stopped on her way to the eggplants.

"Hello there," he said in an offhand sort of voice. As if he couldn't avoid greeting her but wished he could.

"Hello," said Grace. "I just got told off because you left Woof blocking the store doorway."

"Why you?" he asked, raising an eyebrow.

"The woman thought he was mine because I patted him."

"Perhaps you'd better not touch him," said Harry. He moved away and Grace turned her back and picked out two large eggplants. She continued on to the dairy section for a package of grated cheese and then selected the meat she needed, mentally ticking off items in her head for the recipe. That was all. She stood in the checkout line.

Harry came and stood behind her. Grace unloaded her groceries on to the conveyor belt. She could see Woof looking anxiously in through the sliding doors. He was sitting right in the middle now and people were edging around him warily.

"I think he's in the way," she said to Harry.

"He's worried I've abandoned him. He's very loyal."

"That's terribly inconsiderate. Someone might trip over him."

"Save my spot," he said and handed her his laden basket.

Grace watched him push through the crowded checkout and move an excited, welcoming Woof to the side out of sight. She put his basket on the floor.

"Satisfied?" he asked tersely when he returned. Grace nodded. Was she overdoing it and being plain rude instead of assertive? She couldn't judge. People like that always sounded rude in her opinion.

The checkout girl began swiping Grace's purchases and as she pushed them along Grace glanced at the cheese. The use by date was yesterday. Her immediate reaction was "don't bother, it should be all right." Instead, New Grace said, "Excuse me, this cheese is out of date."

The girl inspected it, then inspected Grace. Her name badge said Cheryl. She pursed her lips, turned the bag over again.

"One day," she said. "It looks all right."

Grace steeled herself for an all out brawl. Cheryl had the look of a fighter and must be an expert at dealing with picky customers. But Grace wasn't backing down now. "It's out of date. It shouldn't be on the shelf."

"I suppose not. Must have been overlooked. Sorry." Cheryl eyed her blankly. Waited a moment. Grace eyed her right back. Cheryl said, "Would you like to get another one?"

"Yes. Thank you. I will."

Harry stepped aside for her.

"What?" cried the man next in line. "Come on. I haven't got all day and neither has anyone else."

"Sorry," said Grace. "You'll have to wait."

Harry folded his arms, his basket at his feet. He gazed out the door with a far away look on his face

When she returned with more cheese the line had increased and so had the grumbles. Grace held her head high and pushed her way through with Kirsty's voice singing in her head, "I am woman hear me roar!"

She checked the receipt the girl handed her to make sure she hadn't paid for two packages of cheese. Harry and Cheryl smiled at each other as she weighed his mango.

Grace left the supermarket with pride. Of course, she'd never be brave enough to set foot in the place again when that girl was on the checkout and she'd have to duck around the corner out of sight if she saw that cranky woman who thought she owned Woof—but she'd asserted herself.

Going about annoying and irritating people was a very upsetting way to live life. Grace's legs felt wobbly on the way home. Delayed shock, she decided. Harry and Woof were strolling along half a block ahead. Harry was whistling. They stopped so that Woof could sniff a lamppost and Grace caught up to them. She kept walking.

Woof bounded across to her, tail wagging frantically but Harry snapped his fingers and said, "Heel," so sharply Woof skidded to a halt.

"Sorry," said Harry tersely. "I know you don't like dogs. Unfortunately he seems to like you."

Grace gave him a tight little smile and strode on. What an impression she was making! A dog-hating, argumentative, nit-picking, complaining, unfriendly, unneighborly pain in the butt. And he seemed such a nice man. With such a gorgeous dog. She stopped suddenly and turned to face Harry. Old Grace made a brief resurgence.

"Would you like to have dinner with us tonight?" she asked. He looked as surprised as she was to have blurted out the invitation. "I'm making moussaka."

"I'm afraid I'm busy," he said after a moment's pause.

Grace nodded. Not surprising given her antics in his presence. She began to walk again and he caught her up.

"I lecture on Thursday evenings," he said.

"I see." Grace nodded again. Good enough excuse. Could be true. Disappointing though, surprisingly so.

"You've been practicing a lot lately," commented Harry.

"Does it bother you?" Was he about to complain about her when his dog made that unholy racket?

"It has great penetration power," he said.

"I'm not going to stop practicing, you know. It's my profession."

"I know."

They walked in silence until Harry said, "I work in a room on the far side and you're not a beginner, thank heavens. That would be hard to take."

"I hear Woof," she said and when he didn't comment she added, "I'm practicing for an audition. To move up to second desk. I'm fourth desk at the moment."

"I could never understand that desking thing. Don't you all play the same music?"

"Yes but ranking is important," said Grace. "It's a matter of pride and status. The closer to the front you sit the more respect you have from the other players."

Harry pursed his lips and nodded. "I see."

"A lot of people will be trying out for that position. I have to work really hard."

"You sound very good to me but then what do I know?" said Harry and laughed.

"Exactly," said Grace, annoyed by his offhand reaction and the way he obliquely complained about her music and the way he made her seem like Edward. She even sounded like Edward. "I am a good player and I want to get that second desk chair."

"I wish you luck," he said mildly.

"Luck has nothing to do with it," said Grace. "It's hard work and talent that get you where you want to go in life. No good sitting about waiting for the grass to grow." She'd got that from Jeremy. He said it all the time.

They walked on slowly. Harry said, "I thought if I keep Woof indoors when you practice we might be okay. Seems to be working."

Grace said, "Not really but I ignore him when he starts. Although we've finished with that orchestral piece he really hated. Thank goodness," she added.

If Harry was offended or upset by her comment about Woof he didn't show it.

"Don't like it?" he asked.

"We all hate it with a passion. It's garbage and the man's such a poseur. He wrote a piece for violin which is absolutely ghastly." Old Grace cowered while New Grace gave vent to feelings usually only shared with

Eric, and mildly at that. Her general attitude had always been just play it and put up with it and let the others complain. Not any more.

"What is it?"

" 'Sea Dreaming' by Roger Handley." She laughed. "Eric calls it 'Sea Drowning.' "

"I know Roger," said Harry calmly.

Grace closed her eyes briefly and took a deep breath. She might have known that would happen. But she was entitled to her opinion and just because Harry knew the composer didn't mean she should change her mind. He hadn't had to play the thing or listen to it. Woof appreciated what she meant.

"Really?" she said.

"Really," he said. "Went to school with him."

Woof shoved his nose into her hand and she gave him a surreptitious little pat. He liked her even if Harry didn't.

"He was a real pain in the neck then, too," Harry said.

Grace glanced across at him quickly but he didn't look at her, just kept walking with his shopping bag swinging from his hand and his face an impassive mask, in profile.

Chapter Three

Harry grilled himself a steak for dinner after shutting Woof outside in the garden. His class started at seven thirty and he preferred to eat first. Janis had hated his evening lectures because it meant they didn't see each other much and she had to organize a sitter for William. She rarely made the effort to get home before seven but her career in advertising was a different and far more important matter than his as a lowly tertiary educator.

She accused him of volunteering for the late classes and in the end she'd been right. Anything to get away from her nagging. Since the divorce and in the absence of William he was glad he had to go out at night, helped fill the empty hours.

His mind swung next door. To the odd assortment of

people living in that house. Grace didn't seem to fit in at all, she was far too prickly and petty yet they appeared to have been sharing happily for several years and both men were obviously fond of her. Woof liked her, too.

Harry mentally shrugged. He didn't want to concern himself with that woman. She was too uncomfortable a reminder of Janis. Same driving ambition and lack of feminine warmth. Except every now and then he got a flashback to how she looked standing forlornly in her pink, Chinese robe at the front gate. He'd meant what he'd said so spontaneously. She did look lovely. Yet she seemed like a different person now. Maybe Marcel was right and she was upset by the demise of her relationship. He could relate to that. But both of them were better off without their respective exes. And he was certainly not about to become entangled with another woman, not with William to be considered.

On the way home from class that night Harry remembered with a thrill of pleasurable anticipation that he was picking William up tomorrow after school and bringing him home to Curston Road for his first night in the new house. Of course, he'd been to the place before. Harry had told him that his input into the gigantic decision of which house to buy was every bit as important as his own. William had taken it very seriously and together over many a weekend they had pondered and rejected and wrinkled their brows and rolled their eyes until both had instantly smiled at the sight of this house with its rose lined front path and spacious back garden with two birches, a lemon tree and flower beds. William chose one of the three bedrooms and announced that this was the house to buy.

On Friday afternoon he rushed inside with Woof bounding at his side.

"See, Dad," he exclaimed. "Told you this was the best house."

"You were right," said Harry. "But I agreed with you, remember."

William darted about like a small whirlwind checking where everything was, that all his possessions had been transferred from Harry's small rented flat.

"You've bought a new table," he announced as he appeared in the kitchen.

"Had to, otherwise we'd be eating off the floor."

Harry placed a plate of hot buttered raisin toast on said table. William opened the fridge and took out a carton of milk to pour himself a glass. He cleared the plate in minutes, licking butter off his fingers, slurping milk and Harry silently watched every move he made.

"Dad?"

"Yes?"

"What can we do now?" William sat back with a satisfied sigh. Woof rested his head on his thigh and gazed hopefully into his face.

"I've got some work to do," said Harry. "How about you take Woof out the back?"

"Can I take him for a walk?"

"Not until you get to know the area," said Harry. "We'll go later."

"Okay." A scramble of paws and a rush of bodies and feet and they were gone.

Harry stacked the plates and glass and went to the room he'd turned into his study. He had essays to mark but he also had an idea burning in his mind for his new book. He'd already jotted down some notes but somehow another twist to the story had emerged and he had to write before he lost it. And it was quiet at the moment. No violin, no howling.

Grace went out to bring in her washing and a tennis ball sailed over the fence and bounced across the lawn. She picked it up but dropped it quickly. It was wet and unpleasant to the touch, almost slimy. She looked towards Harry's yard. He must be throwing a ball for Woof.

"Excuse me." That wasn't Harry's voice. Far too high. Grace walked across to the fence stepping carefully through the dahlias, and looked over. A small boy was peering through the cracks between the palings. He had fair hair and blue eyes and looked up at her with a shy smile. At a guess she'd say he was about eight or nine.

"Hello," she said. "My name's Grace. Who are you?"

"William Birmingham," he replied promptly. "And this is Woof."

"I've already met Woof," said Grace and smiled. "He's a lovely dog."

"My ball slipped when I was throwing it for him and it went into your yard. Can I have it back, please?"

"So that's why it's all wet and yucky," said Grace and laughed.

William laughed too. "It's his favorite game and he gets slobbery when he's excited."

Grace walked back and gingerly picked up the ball between thumb and forefinger. She dropped it over the fence. Woof immediately made a dash for it and then ran about with it between his teeth.

"Are you visiting?" asked Grace.

"Just for the weekends. I'm allowed to stay at holidays too but I come more than that. Mom works a lot. Dad and I chose this house."

"You're Harry's son?" said Grace in surprise.

"Yes. Didn't you know?"

"No. I don't know your Dad very well. He's only just moved in."

"Oh yes," said William. He ran after Woof. "See you later," he tossed over his shoulder to Grace and she, dismissed, went back to her laundry basket.

Harry had a child. One child? More? William hadn't mentioned any siblings. Harry had a wife. Had had a wife and William now lived with her. Sad for them both. Grace hated to hear about marriages breaking up and children having to shuttle between the two exes. If she ever had children she'd make sure . . . Grace stopped, unsure how to continue that line of thought. She couldn't even maintain a relationship let alone one involving children. Nobody went into marriage expecting it to fall apart. Nobody willingly gave up their children unless they were in desperate straits or the worst type of unfeeling monster. It was all very sad.

"Grace is nice," said William out of the blue the next morning when he and Harry walked to the shops.

"Grace from next door?" asked Harry in amazement.

"Yes."

"How do you know her?"

"She gave my ball back. Can I have an icecream, please?"

"Yes."

William liked Grace, Woof liked Grace. Eric and Marcel liked Grace. Was he missing something?

"I'm going to learn Italian," Grace announced a few days later when she and Eric were chewing their way through another of Marcel's curries. He'd made an effort to vary it this time by reading a recipe from one of Grace's numerous cookbooks. Even he was getting tired of chicken curry and had successfully mastered a Malaysian style Beef Rendang, to his proud surprise and their relief.

"Where?" asked Eric.

"Why?" asked Marcel.

"At the community center. Classes have already started but the teacher said it wasn't too late to join in."

Grace looked at Marcel. "I want to do something different. Expand myself."

He nodded wisely. "The new Grace. Great language Italian, has the rhythm of life, pulses with passion and lust. Italians don't hide their emotions they let it all hang out. Love, hate, pride, sorrow. Like jazz."

"Like opera," said Eric and winked at Grace as Marcel rose to the bait and began a vehement and oft repeated diatribe about the ludicrous and contrived nature of grand Italian opera, finishing with, "And it's so boring, man!"

The Italian classes were held in meeting room No 3 at the local Community and Arts Center. Grace had once attended aerobics there in the main gym which was also used as a theater. Once being the operative word. It was all too loud and vigorous and enthusiastic and she decided half way through a complicated pattern of steps and arm waving stretches done to a pounding rock beat that aerobics wasn't her thing. She didn't want to become part of the sweatband and purple lycra brigade either. Tai Chi and yoga looked more her style by the information on the brochures stuck to the noticeboard but she'd never manage to fit a regular class into her orchestral schedule. Italian at ten on Monday mornings was perfect. They rarely rehearsed on Monday mornings.

Grace arrived a few minutes early in order to introduce herself to the teacher but he hadn't arrived so she joined the three other people sitting around two large tables pushed together in the center of the room. They were chatting quietly and looked up as she came in.

"Excuse me. Is this Italian lessons?" she asked.

"*Si, si, buon giorno*," answered a thin, balding man and beamed proudly. "*Mi chiamo Roberto*."

"*Buon giorno*. Hello," said Grace. "I'm Grace. Is that what you said?" Even she could tell his accent was atrocious. "You're Roberto?"

"*Si*," he said. "Robert actually but Roberto in Italian." He chuckled in a jovial, scout master manner. "We take on our Italian personas here. Try to live the language. Immerse ourselves."

"Hello Grace. I'm Lydia and this is my husband John," said the woman sitting opposite Roberto.

"Giovanni," interrupted Roberto. John nodded to her and Grace smiled at them. Both retired and improving their minds, she guessed. It was hard to tell why Roberto was here and why he wasn't at work. No doubt he'd tell her if she asked. Lydia and John looked nice, friendly, like the memories and photographs she had of her grandparents. Lydia wore a pastel blue dress which matched her silvery gray hair. John had half glasses for reading perched on his nose. And false teeth.

"Are you just starting today?" Roberto asked. "This is our third lesson." He looked worried on her behalf which was kind of him but then he said, "I hope it doesn't hold us up." And Grace made a rapid reassessment and swallowed the apology which had risen spontaneously to her lips.

New Grace said coolly, "Yes. I hope I haven't missed too much but the man I spoke to said it would be all right. Franco, is it?"

"Franco, it is," said Roberto. "And here's our illustrious *professore*, right now. *Ciao* Franco."

Franco burst into the room like a tornado.

"*Ciao*, Roberto. *Ciao* Lydia and Giovanni. You must be Grace?"

Somehow he gave the impression of being on the verge of falling apart, like a giant stuffed toy whose seams were bursting open. He carried a briefcase which he dumped loudly on the table along with a cellular phone and car keys which skidded off the vinyl surface and clattered onto the wooden floor.

"*Mamma mia,*" he cried and disappeared under the table to emerge red-faced and puffing from the effort of bending over. His knees cracked alarmingly as he bent and straightened. He ran a pudgy hand through thick dark curls. "Sit down, Grace, sit down." Fortissimo sprang to mind. Very loud suited Franco perfectly. She sat down next to Lydia.

"We have another new friend joining us today so you will not be alone," he bellowed enthusiastically accompanying the words with a big smile displaying crooked teeth.

Three more people came in and sat around the table.

A shy, young pregnant woman called Liz—"Elisabetta," announced Roberto—a middle aged French woman, Claudette, and Myra. Claudette and Myra, Roberto left alone. Grace looked at Myra with a vague and uneasy sense of recognition.

Myra wore a long, flowing, red patterned skirt, a white scoop necked gypsy style blouse, a red scarf knotted about her long, gray streaked auburn hair which either trailed down her back or flopped over her shoulder when she turned her head, and silver dangling ear rings depicting celtic crosses. Myra was at least sixty. Myra had rings galore on her fingers and, in her Indian leather sandals and with her vague air of distraction, was what could be classed as an eccentric. Grace had an eerie feeling she could be looking at herself in thirty years time. Correction—Old Grace in thirty years time. Lonely and maybe even slightly loopy.

Myra said, "Hello" in an airy, arty, other worldly voice and Grace imagined she gave palm readings and communed with the spirit world. That, even Old Grace drew the line at. Myra gave her a penetrating and unnerving stare from her dark eyes. Perhaps she did mind readings. Grace hastily stopped herself thinking Myra was loopy. Lovely earrings. She'd always been partial to celtic artwork herself and hadn't been able to stop wearing her favorite rings and ethnic earrings in favor of small gold studs or pearls.

Franco looked around the group. "Just waiting on our other new student." Grace caught the annoyed expression which flitted across Robert's face. So did Franco apparently because he said, "*Come stai,* Giovanni? Lydia?"

"*Bene grazie,* Franco."

Franco opened his briefcase and scattered books and papers in all directions. Claudette clamped her hand on a sheaf before it cascaded to the floor. Liz threw Grace an amused little smile. The door opened and Franco yelled, "Aha. *Buon giorno, buon giorno.* Please come in. This is our other new classmate. Everyone meet Harry Birmingham."

"The writer?" asked John and stood to offer Harry his hand. Roberto muttered to Grace, "*The* writer? Never heard of him."

"Neither had I," said Grace quietly. What on earth was Harry doing here? He was supposed to be writing. At home. Cranking out his science fiction. Now he'd be sitting there with his all seeing eyes judging everything she did and said. He popped up everywhere.

Harry's gaze fell on Grace. She should be at a rehearsal, surely! Darned woman sitting there primly in her gray skirt and white blouse like some escapee from an insurance company or an advertising agency. Like Janis. Starched and stiff and demanding. Judging him with those cool eyes and finding him wanting. He turned his attention to John who was telling him how much he'd enjoyed his latest release and how pleased he was it was up for an award.

"Thank you," Harry said and pulled out a chair next

to a young pregnant woman who cast him a quick shy glance then looked away.

"I think we will start," said Franco. "*Ben venuto*, Grace and Harry."

"*Grazie*," they said together.

"Please introduce yourselves one by one, starting with Liz."

The class progressed slowly. Grace learned how to ask someone's name and respond with her own, how to ask after someone's health and answer accordingly and then discovered how complex Italian verb structures were. She was delighted when Franco praised her accent but said nothing to Harry who seemed to have trouble getting his tongue around the rolling 'r' sound.

"Rrrrr," roared Franco sounding like a deafening version of Brandy purring when she was patted.

"Eerr," struggled Harry sounding indecisive for the first time in Grace's short acquaintance with him. She felt childishly superior and gave him a smug smile which he ignored.

Franco called a brief break at eleven and they straggled out to the foyer area where a little café served tea and cakes.

"*Una cappuccino, prego,*" said Roberto. "Allow me to buy you a cup of coffee Grace. Grazia, I should say. That would be your Italian name."

"Thank you very much," said Grace.

"*Grazie,* Grazia. Remember we must constantly practice so that the language becomes completely natural to us."

"Of course. *Grazie,* Roberto," said Grace. What a completely natural bore the man was but Grace smiled and took her cup and followed him to a table already occupied by Myra and Liz. The others crowded about the counter collecting refreshments. Franco plonked himself down at their table and with him, Harry.

"Now, tell me why you want to learn Italian, Grace," said Franco fixing her with the two dark brown eyes lurking beneath his tousled head of curls.

"I wanted to do something different," she said. She could hardly say she wanted to make herself more interesting as a person—to men. "Italian is the language of music. It's always appealed to me, the sound of it. I'm a musician," she added. Myra was watching her intently, holding her mug of herbal tea in both hands as if it were a crystal ball. Reading her mind?

"What do you play?" asked Lydia from the next table.

"Violin. I'm with the City Symphony."

"Aaah," breathed Myra as if it confirmed something she'd suspected all along.

"We go to all their concerts," said Lydia, delighted and obviously impressed. "I thought you looked familiar, didn't I, John?"

"Giovanni," piped up Robert obviously feeling left out.

"Did you, dear?" asked John. He picked up his tea cup.

"No wonder you have such a good ear for the language," said Franco enthusiastically. "Italian is a very musical language. Full of passion and love. What about you, Harry? Why are you joining our class?"

Yes indeed, Harry.

"Are you going to put us in your next book?" asked Robert with a slight edge to his voice. Harry glanced at him and smiled.

"No, no. My reason is similar to Grace's but I'm planning a trip to Italy next year and thought I'd prepare myself."

"That's why we're here too," said Lydia. "Aren't we Jo . . . Giovanni?" She threw Robert a tight little smile.

"*Si,*" said Giovanni and took a bite out of his shortbread biscuit.

So—Harry was going to Italy?

"What will you do with Woof?" blurted Grace.

Harry looked at her in surprise. He shrugged. "William wants to take him."

"Oh, of course." Grace subsided into her seat and sipped her cappuccino.

"Do you two know each other?" asked Robert suspiciously.

"We're neighbors," said Grace in case he began to concoct conspiracy theories. "Harry only moved in a week or two ago. We barely know each other."

Franco looked at Robert. "Why are you wanting to learn Italian, Roberto?" he asked.

"I've always wanted to read Dante in the original," Robert replied grandly and Grace nearly laughed out loud. No wonder he'd never heard of Harry the sci fi writer. She caught Harry's eye inadvertently while trying not to cackle, and a spark of something flew between them. His face was impassive and he shifted his gaze from her to Robert but Grace knew his reaction had been exactly the same as hers.

"A marvellous ambition," cried Franco encouragingly. "Dante Alighieri, a genius of Italian literature. What about you, Liz?"

"I'm trying to stop my brain going soft from having children," she said quietly. "Sometimes I think my conversational powers have stalled at preschool level."

"Do you have other children?" asked Harry.

"One. She's three and I leave her in day care for a couple of hours and come here. It's so nice to talk to adults again. I'm actually a biologist by training." She blushed pink and stared at her empty tea cup.

"I'm afraid our Italian conversational skills are only at preschool level," said John suddenly and everyone laughed.

"Myra?" asked Franco.

"I was Italian in a past life," she announced dramatically.

This time Grace had to seriously clench her teeth together and dig her nails into her palms. She didn't dare look at Harry. Robert had no such scruples or was it tact he was lacking?

"Garbage!" he said. "Utter nonsense all that past life mumbo jumbo."

"Do not speak of that of which you know nothing," said Myra and gave him a steely stare from her dark eyes. "Grace understands." Now they bored into Grace's very soul.

Grace gulped and nearly choked on her giggles. Harry murmured, "Good heavens."

"Grazia understands, as do we all, that it's new age nonsense!" asserted Robert. He smiled ingratiatingly at Grace.

"I think it is time we continued," said Franco hastily and the group clattered chairs and gathered up belongings and went back to Meeting Room No 3.

At twelve, the class finished. Grace said *'Ciao'* to her new classmates and headed for the street door.

"Would you like a ride home?"

Grace stopped. Harry looked as if he didn't care one way or the other. Grace considered the options. A twenty minute walk complete with one very steep hill going up this time, waiting fifteen minutes for a bus or riding with Harry and getting home in five minutes.

"Yes, please," she said.

They walked around to the parking area at the back of the community center. Harry had a white Holden station wagon with a grill across the back section for Woof to ride behind. He opened the door for Grace and closed it for her as well when she was inside. He backed out and drove to the street where they waited for a break in the traffic.

"How about Myra?" he said casually, peering to the left.

Grace gave a snort of laughter. "What I'd like to know is, if she was Italian in a past life . . ."

"Why can't she already speak Italian?" finished Harry for her. "Did you 'understand'?" he asked in a portentous voice and then added, "Rather fascinating woman, I thought."

"You don't believe in past lives, do you?" cried Grace, although it was an intriguing concept—not something to actually believe in but interesting all the same. The sort of thing at which Jeremy scoffed even more than Robert. New Grace was far too businesslike to dabble in the supernatural. "And believe me I understand nothing. She's quite peculiar, that woman." And just a bit scary with her dark-eyed stares.

"I write sci fi, remember? Things like that are interesting."

"I tend to agree with Robert," said Grace. "Do you think he'll get to the stage of reading Dante?"

"Roberto, remember Grazia. How are you ever going to learn if you keep forgetting to think in Italian?" said Harry sternly. His eyes flicked towards her, smiling.

Grace crossed her legs and tugged her skirt down as far as she could. This skirt was awkward and embarrassingly revealing. Harry must be getting a real eyeful.

How she longed for her comfortable Fijian wraparound or her purple harem pants. Wrong! Wrong! Wrong!

A vision of herself at Myra's age swam dizzyingly and frighteningly before her eyes. She would not end up like that, going round alarming unsuspecting people with her wild statements from the other side and dressed like a leftover hippy from the sixties. A grown up, wrinkled, flower child.

But! Women had a right to wear what they liked and not be judged for it and not be made to feel they were being provocative and temptresses. Otherwise, Grace decided, she'd end up wearing a totally concealing veil like those women under the oppressive Taliban regime. Myra had every right to dress as she pleased, too. Laughing behind her back was cruel.

"We shouldn't make fun of them," she said.

"No," said Harry. The uptight Grace had made a rapid reappearance. For a minute there he'd almost warmed to her. Mustn't make that mistake. A woman with multiple personalities was a definite no-no. Maybe William had come across the mild one. He'd only spoken to her briefly after all.

Harry swung into his driveway and turned off the engine. Grace opened her door before he could get around to her side. Mustn't make that mistake either, treating her with old-fashioned courtesy. She was liable to snap at him the way Janis did before he learnt to let her open her own doors and carry her own bags.

"Thanks for the lift," she said.

"No trouble. See you next week." Harry turned and walked to his front door. Grace was already on the footpath in front of their houses.

"Good bye," she called.

Harry went straight through the house to open the door to the back garden. Woof didn't come bounding up to him as he expected. He called. No response. Harry ran across the yard to the back fence and checked behind the trees and shrubs. No loose palings, no holes in the ground where a dog might have dug his way out like an escaping POW. He checked the side fence where he'd replaced the broken slats. All in order. The other side. Secure. Harry stood in the middle of the garden and stared around, totally perplexed. He walked to the side of the house and round to the fence behind the carport. The gate was closed and padlocked but there was a telltale tuft of grey fur on the top wire. The devil had jumped the fence.

Harry groaned and then cursed. Woof could be anywhere. He could be flattened on the road or lying hurt. Stolen, even. Woof was a valuable dog, a Malamute with a pedigree Harry could wallpaper the spare room with.

He went next door to Grace's house. Woof had visited before. He may have done so again. Grace opened the door.

"Woof's gone," he said without preamble. Grace frowned.

"Where?" she said.

"If I knew that I wouldn't be here," snapped Harry.

"Well, I haven't seen him I was with you, remember?"

"I'm sorry I bothered you." Harry turned away. "I might have known you wouldn't care," he muttered as he hurried down the path. A hollow feeling, dread, yawned inside. Where was Woof? He could have travelled miles in the time Harry had been absent.

Grace watched him stride away and had a flash of dejá vu—only last time it was Jeremy striding away, furious with her. She'd managed to do it again. Infuriate a man without trying. And Harry was being grossly unfair just like Jeremy. Of course she cared about Woof. He could be getting run over by a car or running around annoying and frightening people by being friendly. He was so big a child could be very intimidated. Woof could get into all sorts of trouble through no fault of his own. As he'd done by pushing through the fence and squashing Marcel's vegetables. He was just being a dog. He should be cared for and protected from himself.

Grace ran down the path and yelled, "You should shut him in properly. You're really irresponsible, you know that?"

Harry spun around and strode back to where she stood at the lopsided gate.

"Don't you tell me what's responsible. Women like you . . . You're exactly like my ex-wife. All complaints and prickles and not a drop of empathy or sympathy. Very unattractive. No wonder that lawyer fellow dumped you. Men like some softness in a woman."

Grace clenched her hands into fists. Never in her whole life had she experienced such a rush of anger. "No wonder you're divorced. That poor woman was well rid of you."

Harry's eyes bored into hers. "You're exactly the same. Totally self obsessed. Janis should never have had a child and by the look of things it's just as well you don't have any. Women like you are meant to be single."

Grace stared at him totally lost for words at the cruel and hideous enormity of the wrongness of what he was saying. New Grace collapsed in a heap, her anger suddenly extinguished by a rising flood of tears and she raced for the front door. It had closed behind her and locked itself. She rang the bell but of course that didn't achieve anything because it had stopped working six months ago. Eric and Marcel were out anyway. Grace spun round in her watery, confused humiliation and cannoned into Harry who had followed her down the path and now stood right behind her, blocking the escape route.

He held her arms as she tried to push passed him and that meant she couldn't wipe the tears away which had begun overflowing and coursing down her cheeks.

"Grace. I'm sorry," he said and his voice was much quieter and sounded very regretful, the bits she heard through the roaring in her own ears. "I'm really sorry. I shouldn't have said any of that. I . . . I've no excuse, it was unforgivable."

"Yes," mumbled Grace and sniffed hard. He pulled her clumsily against him in a rough hug, his arms firm and warm around her back, then released her and she fumbled in her pocket for a tissue keeping her face averted as she attempted to stem the floodtide. Her hands were trembling.

"I hardly know you. I don't know anything about you to make those comments. I'm sorry."

"Okay," said Grace. She nipped past him and ran blindly across to the side of the house and down the driveway to the back yard. She knew the back door was open, she'd just put some garbage in the trash can. Harry didn't follow her. If he had she would have belted him with the first thing that came to hand. The trash can lid or Marcel's rake propped against the wall.

What had gone wrong? Why had he said those hateful things? Was it her fault for calling him irresponsible? Possibly. He was worried about Woof, she could see that, feeling guilty for allowing him to get out of the yard.

Grace lay flat on her back on her bed. She was doing it again. Justifying someone else's rudeness and twisting it around to make it seem like her fault. In part it was but Harry had no reason to say those things to her and he knew it. He'd apologized immediately. He really didn't know anything about her and she knew nothing about him and wanted to know even less.

Saying she'd be a terrible mother and should never have children. She adored children, had always wanted a child of her own. That was part of her whole despair at being single at thirty. A big uncontrolled sob burst out and she let it go. And saying those things about her being unattractive. Horrible things. How could he say that? He was wrong! Men did find her attractive. He'd said she looked lovely himself when he first saw her in the front garden.

It was after that first attraction wore off she had the trouble. Like now. Grace lay and sobbed and sniffed. Harry was wrong and Harry was horrible.

But where had Woof gone? That lovely, big, friendly, non-judgemental lump of a canine. He might be lost and frightened, wandering about. Grace went to the bathroom and washed her face. She changed her skirt for jeans, collected her keys, stuck them in her pocket and went to help search.

She didn't know where Harry had gone looking and she prayed he'd headed for the shops. That would be logical because Woof had probably been that way more often. Were dogs logical thinkers? In their own doggy way they probably were. Grace turned in the opposite direction and walked around to the other side of the block. She asked a woman watering her garden but Woof hadn't been spied in her street. Grace wandered on, calling and whistling to no avail.

After an hour her stomach told her she'd forgotten lunch. Eric was in the kitchen when she returned, footsore and hot.

"Hi, where have you been?" he said. "How was Italian?"

"Okay," she said. "Woof got out and ran away. Harry was really upset. I went to help look for him."

"He's back," said Eric. "Want a cup of tea. You'd better be quick we have to leave soon. Three o'clock start remember? Dress rehearsal?"

"Woof's back?" Grace sat down abruptly. "How do you know?"

"Saw him as I came home. Harry was busy putting wire netting on the fence. He said Woof jumped over. Apparently when they realize they can do that it's very hard to stop them because those dogs jump really well."

Grace slumped in her chair. Relief washed over her. Woof wasn't squashed on the road or wandering forlorn and lost. Harry wasn't bereaved. Eric placed a cup of tea in front of her.

"Hurry up," he said. "I'm leaving in ten minutes."

Harry finished his makeshift fencelift after lunch, hammering the nails in hard as he tried to block out the sound of his harsh words to Grace which resounded constantly in his head. Woof lolled in the shade of the house and watched with great interest.

"If you can jump that I'll enter you in the Olympics," Harry said to him. Woof grinned cheerfully. The phone rang from inside the house.

Harry wiped his hands on his shorts and went to answer it. Anna's voice said irritably, "Harry for goodness sake, where've you been all morning?"

"And *buon giorno* to you too," he said.

"I wish you'd remember to switch on your answering machine," she grumbled.

"If I do that I have to return people's calls," he replied, only half joking.

"I need to know if you're bringing a guest to the awards dinner. It's Friday night, remember?"

"This Friday?" Completely joking now. Anna always reacted perfectly. After ten years as his agent and friend she still didn't know when he was pulling her leg.

"Harry!" she shrieked and he smiled as he pictured her round, horrified face which always reminded him of a squirrel with glasses.

"Just kidding," he said mildly. "I thought I'd go by myself."

"You'd be safer with someone. Preferably a woman. Camilla's going to be there," she said portentously.

"Oh no," he groaned. Camilla of the insatiable appetite for Harry Birminghams and the empty ring finger. Camilla who wrote mild mannered children's books about rabbits and who was also in the running for an award. Camilla who declared her passion for him when he was still married to Janis and to whom in a weak moment he had admitted his unhappiness over too many champagne cocktails at a book launch. Camilla who now thought her day had come. "I'll find someone," he said.

"Harry Birmingham and guest then," said Anna.

"Yes." Harry hung up wondering who on earth 'and guest' would be. A married female friend? None sprang to mind who weren't really Janis's friends and that could be tense. Lauren from the University English department! She'd enjoy it and she wouldn't read anything extra into the invitation. He riffled through his address book. Lauren was terribly sorry but she was going away next weekend leaving immediately after lunch on Friday.

Harry went into his office and sat at his desk. Who could he ask? He stared vacantly out the window and watched Woof dawdle across the grass and flop down under one of the birches. Thank goodness he was home safe and sound. The big idiot had come lolloping along the path soon after Harry had gone to look for him. Must have headed for the shops and been sidetracked. He had that guilty look on his face when he knew he'd done wrong.

Harry closed his eyes briefly and grimaced as he remembered how excruciatingly rude he'd been to that poor woman next door. No matter what he thought of her there was no excusing the way he'd spoken to her. Pouring all the poison meant for Janis out on her.

Grace. She'd crumpled under his onslaught and the fierce, uptight powerhouse had suddenly become the trembling, forlorn girl he'd first seen in the pink robe on the doorstep. A lovely girl with a soft, bewildered expression and tears in her eyes. That's why he'd hugged her quickly, he'd caught another glimpse of that vulnerable child and wanted to protect her again. From himself, this time.

Perhaps he should ask her to the awards dinner as an apology and an atonement of sorts, show there were no hard feelings from his side. She *was* very attractive, he couldn't imagine where that remark had come from. The sludge of repressed bitterness towards Janis was the only answer. Poor Grace. Harry rubbed his hands over his face and groaned in a belated rush of complete humiliation and embarrassment as he remembered exactly what he'd said to her. Did he have the nerve to face her? He had to for two very good reasons.

One—an abject apology and atonement. He couldn't possibly shirk it however embarrassing it might be.

Two—he needed a date for Friday and Grace would be a good and plausible way of keeping Camilla at bay.

Harry nodded to himself. Good plan and with any luck she'd be free on Friday.

Later that afternoon he went next door. He took another bunch of roses just to make quite sure he looked suitably contrite which he truly was but he left Woof at home knowing her dislike of animals, or at least dogs.

Marcel let him in and offered him Jungle Juice. Bilious green this time. Why, Harry didn't dare ask.

"They'll be home soon," Marcel said and resumed his spot at the kitchen table where the day's newspaper was spread in an untidy mess. He pointed to an advertisement. "See this?" he asked. "Eric Bibb's coming to town. Great blues singer, man. You've gotta see him."

"I have seen him," said Harry. "In the States last year."

"Cool," said Marcel. "Who else did you catch?"

When Grace and Eric came in half an hour later Harry and Marcel were on their second glass of green gunk, which tasted far better than it looked, and an in depth discussion of jazz guitarists and how Harry, according to Marcel, incorporated jazz style, free, creative expressionism into his writing.

"The groove," said Marcel. "It's gotta have the groove, man. All good art has the groove. You've got the groove."

"He's on his groove rave," said Eric over his shoulder to Grace who was obscured behind him and then to Marcel, "What on earth made the JJ go that color?"

"Kiwi fruit," said Marcel. "Or maybe it was the beans."

"Bean juice?" Eric blanched.

Harry stood up as Grace entered the kitchen. She flushed when she saw him and looked away, walking stiffly to the fridge and taking out the bottle of mineral water. She had on jeans now and a floral print blouse. She looked softer and more pliable despite her obvious embarrassment at seeing him here when she least expected to. He indicated the roses Marcel had stuck in a vase and placed on the bench.

"I brought these for you, Grace."

"Thanks," she muttered. Harry stepped closer to her and said softly so that Eric and Marcel who had started arguing about who ate the last of the cheese, wouldn't hear, "I'm really sorry Grace about—earlier. Please forgive me. I was completely out of order. I have no excuse."

Grace faced him then. "I'm sorry, too," she said in a determined voice but her cheeks had a delectable pink glow. "You were worried about Woof. I shouldn't have said what I did."

"I found him."

"Good." She looked about as pleased and interested as if he'd told her it was garbage night.

"You needn't have bothered going looking for him," said Eric who must have been listening after all. Marcel stomped out the back to his garden muttering about watering the tomatoes.

Harry stared at Grace in astonishment. "Did you search for him too?" Grace flushed even pinker and nodded. Harry ran his hand through his hair. "Why?"

"He could've been run over or hurt somewhere."

"But you don't like him."

"I didn't say that." Grace turned away. "I don't like animals in the kitchen and even if I didn't like him I'd hardly want to see him lost or hurt."

Harry leaned against the sink with his arms folded. She was an odd creature. Just when he thought he had her figured out she changed and did something completely out of what he had decided was her character. He never dreamed she would go running about searching for Woof. Especially not after what he'd said to her.

"When's dinner, Grace?" asked Eric.

"It's pasta. It'll take twenty minutes so whenever you like," she said conscious of Harry standing right beside her. Eric disappeared in the direction of his room. Should she invite Harry to stay? Old Grace would. New Grace wasn't so sure. But New Grace was only hanging on by the merest of fingernails at the moment. Roses and an apology were enough to have Old Grace falling over herself but this man had managed to confound and confuse both Graces.

He was making her uncomfortable leaning there calmly, studying her. She felt like an insect. Why was he so amazed that she would look for his dog? His words still resounded in her head despite his humble apology. They'd cut far deeper than he could possibly guess. "Just as well she didn't have a child"—was that true? "Self obsessed?" No-one else thought so or at least no-one had ever said so in such a forthright manner. No-one had ever told her she was unsuitable mother material.

Harry had a very cruel and nasty streak. Grace decided she really didn't want to invite him to eat with them. She wished he'd go home and if he didn't leave soon New Grace would throw him out.

She bent down and opened the vegetable cupboard. Onions and garlic. A chopping board and parsley. Marcel's parsley grew in copious quantities. She stood a pot on the stove top. Olive oil, fresh tomatoes, also Marcel's. Grace wielded the big, sharp knife and it bit into the onion with a satisfying crunch. Go home Harry! She chopped down again.

Harry said, "Would you like to come to an awards dinner with me on Friday night?"

Chapter Four

Grace paused mid hack. She was so surprised her brain momentarily froze and when it did restart the first thing she said was, "Friday?" when what she really meant to say was, "Me? You're asking me?"

"You're probably working," said Harry in an offhand manner. "Or practicing for your audition. Never mind."

"No." Grace began hacking at the onion.

"No what?"

She stopped again and looked at him. "No, we're not working on Friday and I can take a break from practice."

Grace turned back to her mangled onion. Why on earth was he asking her to go out with him? Guilt? It couldn't be because he enjoyed her company because it was patently obvious he didn't. An awards night sounded important. Perhaps he couldn't find anyone else to go with him. Divorced, dateless?—ask the single, uptight woman next-door, make amends for insulting her and making her cry. What on earth made him think she would want to go anywhere with him?

Harry watched a myriad of conflicting emotions wash across her features. She had turned so her face was in profile but he could see the jaw tighten and her lips purse and then relax. She was extraordinarily pretty from this angle and her hair twisted and curled its way out of the pins and clasp with which she'd attempted to control it. A strand fell across her cheek and numerous curls gallivanted heedlessly down over the back of her neck. He had to fold his arms firmly to stop from reaching out and lifting the escaping tendrils from her collar.

"You're mincing that onion," he said.

She knew that. Onion fumes were arrowing their way into her eyes. Grace picked up the chopping board and blindly scraped the onion pieces into the pot. Tears ran down her cheeks.

"Better light the gas," he suggested.

"What's the award?" asked Grace but she did as he said. Then she wiped her face on a hand towel.

"Just some literary thing. You don't have to cry about it."

She ignored that feeble attempt at a joke. "Are you going to win?"

Harry shrugged. "Don't know. One of my books is shortlisted for a sci fi prize."

Grace began cutting up the tomatoes with great precision to forestall any further slurs on her food preparation technique. She sniffed. Her eyes were still watering from the onions.

"Will you come with me?" he asked gently. "Please?"

Why couldn't the woman just say yes or no? Now he was pleading with her and she was debating whether to condescend to lower her standards and be seen out with him. And she was cutting those tomatoes into pedantic little cubes. Harry straightened, prepared to give up and go home before he made a complete fool of himself.

"Yes," said Grace. "I'd like to."

"Oh, okay, Good." Harry smiled and received a tiny twist of the lips in return. "It's formal. At the Hilton. Seven for seven thirty. I'll come over around twenty to."

"All right," said Grace. "Thank you."

"No. Thank *you* or," he frowned momentarily, "*Grazie a Lei.*"

This time Grace smiled a proper smile. "*Prego.*"

"*Ciao*," said Harry and decided to quit while he was ahead.

"Aren't you going out with Harry tonight?" asked Marcel when he came into the living room to get his double bass. He now regularly propped it securely against the wall in the corner, out of the way. "Sounding good, by the way."

"Thanks." Going out? With Harry! It must be Friday!

Grace lowered her bow and glanced at the clock on the mantlepiece. It was always twenty minutes slow. That meant it was . . . Good grief! Twenty to six. An hour to get ready for a formal and important night out. Important to Harry, anyway. What on earth could she wear? New Grace hadn't bought new formal wear yet.

Harry knocked on Grace's door at quarter to seven. His tuxedo felt uncomfortable even though he'd had it for years and wore it occasionally to functions like tonight's. He must be putting on weight because the waistband was tighter than he remembered from last time. These things were such a chore and a bore to go to. If Anna didn't insist and threaten dire consequences he wouldn't attend any of them.

"It's profile maintenance, Harry. Do you want to sell your books?" she said and he had to admit that he did. The yin and yang of being a published writer he supposed. At least Grace would provide protection from Camilla. He'd make sure she stayed close by his side all evening and try not to antagonize her or let her antagonize him.

Harry knocked again, louder. Surely Miss Organized was ready? Marcel's car wasn't in the street out front and neither was Eric's in the driveway. Could she have forgotten and gone off somewhere with them? He thumped on the door with his fist.

"I'm coming," sounded faintly from inside.

Harry relaxed and waited. The door opened and Grace stood there with a flustered expression and wearing . . . what was she wearing? Nothing like what he had expected. Her normal daywear indicated she would choose something straight and plain with spaghetti straps the way Janis did when they went to these formal dinners. Elegant and tasteful with a drop diamond or pearl pendant and matching earrings.

Grace was wearing a garment reminiscent of a Ginger Rogers extravaganza, in deep red satin with long sleeves, ruffles around the neckline and a side split which showed off her legs in sleek, sheer stockings. She'd piled her hair up and stuck a black feather and ruby decoration in it. She looked simply stunning. His face must have registered his complete and utter amazement.

"Is this all right?" she asked. "It's not too . . ."

"It's . . . different," he stammered through his astonishment.

"I can wear one of my black concert things if you think this won't be appropriate," she said.

"Grace, you look marvellous. I love your dress," he said, making a rapid return to coherency. "It's just not what I expected you to wear, that's all."

Grace smiled, her eyes sparkled and Harry's stomach lurched. He felt a leap of unexpected desire, hot and strong. She was a most extraordinary and exciting woman. This version.

"Are you ready?" he asked.

"I'll get my wrap." She disappeared and came back

with an exotic black brocade shawl which she flung over her shoulders.

Harry held the car door open for her again and closed it gently. Grace watched him walk around the front of the car, tall and elegant in his black suit. She was used to the sight of men in their formal wear, most musicians owned a tuxedo, even Marcel. Eric called it his working gear, his overalls. Harry looked as if he'd rather be wearing those old jeans and things he usually wore. Like his shorts. He had good, strong, tanned legs she remembered from the odd glimpse she'd got through the window while practicing and he walked past with Woof.

"You look very smart," she said.

"I think my suit has shrunk since I wore it last," he said.

"When was that?"

"Some publisher's cocktail party I went to with my ex-wife."

"William's a sweet little boy," said Grace a few moments later.

Harry smiled. "He has his moments."

"Must be hard only seeing him at weekends."

"It is."

They drove in silence. Traffic was heavy and they crawled and stopped and crawled and stopped their way into the city center.

"How's the practice going?" he asked while they sat at yet another red light.

"Getting there," she said. "It's hard work. There's some tough competition."

"Why exactly are you doing the audition?" Harry asked.

"To move up a couple of places."

"Is it worth the stress?"

She wondered the same thing at times but then Edward would make some snide remark and she would remember Operation Jeremy and vow to forge ahead.

"I wouldn't be doing it if I didn't think so. Don't you think it's worth trying to improve?"

"I didn't say that." They crawled forward and stopped again. "It seems like a lot of hard work to virtually stay the same."

"I love playing. You work hard, don't you?" challenged Grace.

"Yes. I love what I do, too. But when I write it's not a chore and it doesn't seem like hard work. You just seem to be slogging away for something you already have or at least to get somewhere you're already at. What's the difference where you sit as long as you get to play that fantastic music? You get ulcers like that."

"You've no idea what you're talking about," said Grace loftily. "You must have no ambition."

"I've got six books published," he pointed out.

"Oh," said Grace. "But isn't that because you're good at what you like to do, rather than being really ambitious?"

Harry said, "My ambition is to live a quiet life with

Woof, and preferably William, and write in peace in my new house. And travel to Italy next year. What we're doing now is hard work for me."

"Well, thanks very much!" cried Grace. Not much fun for her either at the moment. She seemed to have talked her way into a position the opposite of what she truly felt.

"No. I mean going to these functions. I'd rather be at home."

"Why accept, then?" asked Grace. If he was nominated for an award the least he could do was be gracious and accept the praise of his peers and fans. Surely that wasn't too difficult.

"It's part of being a successful writer."

"Well don't complain about it. Would you rather be an unsuccessful writer?"

"Of course not." This was exactly the type of conversation he used to have with Janis and she was making it extremely difficult for him to keep to his plan of 'no antagonism.' He might have known she'd revert to this type of behavior. That whole conversation had proved it. Serves him right for being misled by a stunning dress. Harry clenched his teeth and forced his way into the left hand lane, cutting off a taxi whose driver responded with an obscene gesture and a blast on the horn.

Grace stared out the windshield and wondered what sort of fun night she'd let herself in for. If the worst came to the worst she could drink lots of champagne, eat as much as she could and disgrace herself and grouchy Harry would never bother her again.

The elevator doors hissed open on the second floor foyer full of well-dressed people. Waiters circulated with loaded trays and Harry expertly nabbed two tall champagne flutes as one ventured within range.

"*Coraggio*," he murmured and handed a glass to Grace.

"Dutch *coraggio*?" murmured Grace back and he smiled fleetingly and lifted his glass in salute. Grace raised hers.

"Just one," he said. "I'm driving."

She realized with a small shock of surprise that Harry was nervous. He really did hate being here he wasn't just saying it. Her heart melted a tiny bit. She would behave. She would be supportive. She would allow Old Grace a look in. The woman everyone liked. Couldn't hurt for a few hours.

"Thank heavens, you're here at last, Harry," cried a female voice. Its owner reminded Grace of a squirrel. She was round-faced and russet colored and made short, quick, little darting movements with her hands. She smiled at Grace and stuck out one of her little paws.

"I'm Anna Cardew. Harry's long-suffering agent." Hazel eyes twinkled with fondness behind gold rimmed spectacles.

Grace smiled and shook the soft hand, almost expecting a nut to be pressed into her palm.

"Grace Richmond. Harry's neighbor."

"Also long-suffering," put in Harry.

"I love your dress," said Anna, touching the satin

fabric of her sleeve softly. "I couldn't wear something like that. I'd look like I'd raided a theater costume department to play dress-up."

"Thanks, it's one of my favorites but I don't get a chance to wear it much," said Grace. "I like the color you're wearing. Bottle green really suits you."

"Thank you very much!" Anna beamed. "I'm so glad you could come, Grace. Harry's hopeless at these things. He needs a support team. He's going to win, you know," she said confidently. Harry snorted but Grace could tell he was pleased by the little smile on his lips as he looked at the floor.

"Is he?" Grace didn't dare admit she'd never read one of his books and hadn't a clue which book was in the running tonight.

"It's a wonderful book, isn't it? The best yet."

Grace glanced at Harry for help but he just smiled at her enquiringly.

"What's the prize?" she asked.

"A big fat check," said Harry. "Which I could really use after buying that house."

"Plus the kudos. And it translates into fantastic publicity and that generates more sales." Anna the agent smiled happily. "We hope."

"Harry, darling!"

Grace jumped at the shriek of delight right behind her. She held her glass away as champagne slopped over the rim and dripped on to the carpet. A waiter relieved her of it.

"Hello Camilla," said Harry and promptly disappeared behind a blond with a haystack hairdo atop a black, backless frock which slinked its way over rounded hips and fell to the floor in a silky swirl.

Camilla turned with her arm linked through Harry's and silver tipped fingers gripping his wrist. She eyed Grace up and down with a look which would have done credit to an airport custom's official faced with a drug smuggler and then the glittering, blue eyes switched to Anna. A cool, "Hello Anna. Lovely to see you."

Anna responded with, "Likewise" in a very unconvincing manner.

Harry didn't seem to be going to make an introduction or if he was he was taking his time. Or maybe he was trying to breathe through the noxious cloud of perfume which had settled over them with the arrival of the blond. Old Grace would have waited and let this obnoxious woman take charge, but Old Grace had been roughly shoved into the background after her brief appearance for Anna. New Grace stuck out her hand and said, "Hello. Grace Richmond, and you are?"

"Sorry. Camilla Simpson," said Harry, belatedly. "Camilla writes the Ronnie Rabbit books. For children."

"Oh," said Grace. "I'm sorry. I don't know them. I don't have children." She smiled brightly at Camilla and flashed a look at Harry whose lips tightened. "Are you up for an award too?" Camilla didn't look as though she knew what a child was. A less likely looking writer for children she had yet to see.

"Yes," said Camilla in a high, brittle voice. "Children's Book of the Year."

"Goodness. Congratulations and good luck," said Grace.

"Thank you," said Camilla. Grace was dismissed with a turn of the head. Camilla's expression altered and her voice dropped several tones as she said, "Harry you must come and meet Sidney Overall. He's dying to meet you." She began to move away, tossing, "Excuse us," over her shoulder as she dragged at Harry.

Harry pulled his arm free.

"Grace?" he extended his hand, indicating she should go first. Camilla turned with a dangerous glint in her eye. Anna made good her escape with a little wave and a roll of the eyes.

"Oh you're together? I didn't realize. You're so unlike Ja . . . I mean . . . I'm sorry." She stopped and gave Harry a little smile and a look of remorse. "Perhaps some other time."

Grace knew she wasn't sorry at all. She was a lioness on the prowl and Harry was her prey. Grace was, in her eyes, a very minor obstacle. A baby lamb. New Grace would see about that! No blond bimbo was going to home in on her date, her man. The fact that she didn't want Harry herself was irrelevant. She needed all the practice she could get if she was to hunt with the lions.

Grace tucked her hand into Harry's arm. Harry looked down at her with a very surprised expression but she squeezed her fingers surreptitiously and he grinned.

"I know what you mean," Grace said to Camilla. "It's taken us by surprise as well, hasn't it, sweetheart?"

She stretched up and kissed Harry's cheek. The skin was smooth, freshly shaven and he smelled good. She had to place her hand lightly on his chest to steady herself. She could feel the warmth of his body through the dress shirt. His heart was thumping along solidly.

"It certainly has," he murmured after a moment. "Quite a thunderclap."

"Love at first sight," cried Grace gaily, warming to the theme. Her hand didn't seem to want to leave the front of his shirt. She had to consciously remove it but it went and joined the other holding Harry's arm. He placed one hand on both of hers and his fingers clasped firmly. A little shiver of something ran up her spine.

"How wonderful," croaked Camilla. "You must excuse me. I see someone I really must . . ." She pecked Harry on the cheek and skewered Grace with blue icepicks before disappearing into the throng.

"Love at first sight?" asked Harry in a disbelieving voice but he didn't disengage himself from her clutches the way he had from Camilla's. And his eyes were soft as they met hers.

"I thought you needed some protection," said Grace. He removed his hand from on top of hers. "Unless of course, you didn't want protecting." She reluctantly let her fingers slip from his arm and took a glass of orange juice from a hovering waiter.

"I think I need full body armor," he said grimly.

"She's been after me for ages. Even before Janis and I split."

"Not your type?" asked Grace. What was his type?

"No," said Harry with great firmness.

Grace sipped her juice and stared around the room. It was packed now and the roar of conversation almost drowned out the string quartet playing in one corner. Fragments of the *Elizabethan Serenade* floated by accompanied by laughs and occasional comprehensible snippets of talk. She wondered if any of her favorite authors were here. A woman stopped on her way by, said, "Fabulous dress," and moved on before Grace could respond. She caught Harry's eye and smiled, pleased.

"It is," said Harry. "Very sexy."

Grace didn't know whether he was kidding or not. He didn't look as if he was, his expression was completely neutral, may as well have been discussing the color of the carpet, which, she noticed as she glanced down to avoid his increasingly embarrassing scrutiny, was pale gray. Where was the self assured New Woman now? Harry, if he put his mind to it could be completely and unnervingly attractive.

"What's your book called?" she asked. She looked up. Harry was still gazing at her, making her still more uncomfortable. He smiled sending a rush of warmth up her neck. He leaned forward and whispered in her ear, his warm breath tickling her cheek.

"*Time Line.*"

He drew away and his eyes were soft and he was incredibly desirable all of a sudden. Too much champagne? Only a few sips before she'd spilled it. Her heart was beating hard and loud all of a sudden, too. She couldn't believe how touching him had created such internal turmoil.

"What's it about?" Her voice came out quieter than she expected. Harry had to lean forward again to hear her. He stepped closer so their bodies were a shiver apart. His fingers teased a coil of hair on her neck. Her heart nearly stopped.

"I'll lend you a copy." He had her captured with his eyes. Grace held her breath. What was happening here? This was Harry who thought she was all sorts of a pain in the behind. And who she thought was—what did she think?

"Grace! I thought it was you!"

"Jeremy!"

If she'd thought at all she might have guessed he'd be here. He had so many contacts, a finger in many a pie and loved these sorts of elaborate showcase functions. She'd accompanied him to a movie premiere, two theater opening nights and various legal affairs in the last few months.

Jeremy gave Harry an appraising look. "I don't believe we've met," he said, clearly not recognizing the man with the dog who'd peed on his car tire that fateful morning. "Jeremy Forde."

"Harry Birmingham." They shook hands briefly.

"Harry's up for an award. Science Fiction. His book is called *Time Line*," babbled Grace. Jeremy was looking at her the way he used to when they first met. That appraising stare filled with admiring approval of what he saw. His eyes still caused her major internal upheavals. His tuxedo fitted him perfectly, his dress shirt was new and instead of a bow tie he wore the trendy pearl stud at the throat. Quite simply he was just as gorgeous as always. New Grace wasn't ready for a confrontation yet. She hadn't fully prepared her battle plan, was still on preliminary maneuvres. And Harry had ambushed her senses. Old Grace fluttered into the spotlight.

"Congratulations," Jeremy said to Harry in his smooth lawyer's voice. He regarded Grace with a practised eye. "You look absolutely marvellous, Grace." His expression told her she had just made a spectacular reentry to his world.

"Thank you, you look well, too," said Grace and knew her face was as red as her dress.

"What brings you here tonight?" asked Harry in a polite voice.

"My law firm represents a publishing house," said Jeremy. "I wangled a ticket. I like to keep up with the arts. The latest trends etcetera. Who I should be reading and so on." He gave a little, self-effacing chuckle and glanced at Grace. "Grace is the true artist. My actual area of expertise is criminal law but she taught me a lot about the music scene. Got to keep up the contacts or the next guy passes you and leaves you behind."

Harry nodded. "Grace feels the same way. Did you know she's working hard to move up in the orchestra?"

"Are you?" Jeremy looked at Grace with renewed interest.

"It's a second desk position," said Grace.

"Excellent! I'm really glad to hear you've decided to push that talent you've got. She's a very good violinist, you know, Harry, but she never had enough ambition."

"I know she's good," said Harry mildly. "I've heard her play. A lot."

"Have you?" asked Jeremy. He paused and Grace watched him wondering how Harry had managed that. Wondering just what her relationship was with Harry. Could he be just the teensiest bit . . . jealous? Was her plan succeeding already? Was evidence of ambition what turned Jeremy on? Would she be more interesting to him now? He opened his mouth to say something. She smiled to encourage him.

"Yes." Harry took Grace's arm gently. "I think we should go in and sit down now, sweetheart. Nice to meet you, Jeremy."

Harry smiled sweetly at Grace and she managed to say, "Bye Jeremy," before she was led towards the main function room where people were being directed to places at elaborately set tables.

"Sweetheart?" Grace asked indignantly.

"Yes, darling?" said Harry tucking her hand firmly into his arm.

"Harry!" She tried to release her hand but he hung on too tightly.

"Ah there's Anna." He headed across the room with Grace in tow to a round table seating ten people. Anna introduced her husband, Michael and then the others who seemed to be from Harry's publishing firm. His editor was a burly, jovial man called Clive but Grace missed the significance and the names of the rest. Her mind was elsewhere. With Jeremy.

When they were settled and conversations had resumed, Grace said quietly to Harry, "What do you think you were doing?"

"When?"

"Back there, with Jeremy."

"Offering protection, returning the favor," he said calmly.

"What if I didn't want protection?" she whispered fiercely.

"But you did, surely?" Harry asked in a surprised voice. "Isn't he the guy from the street that time? The one who yelled . . ."

"Yes, yes, it is," Grace cut in quickly.

"Well . . . I don't understand," said Harry, clearly bewildered. "Why would you want to talk to him after what he said to you?"

"Yes, well, I'm talking to *you* aren't I?" retorted Grace. "Call me a forgiving person."

Harry firmed his lips into a line and flapped open his napkin. “Sorry,” he said but didn’t sound it.

Grace sipped her glass of iced water. Now Jeremy would disappear again, just when he’d seemed to be interested. Why couldn’t she have been cool and distant instead of blushing furiously like a schoolgirl? The idea was to make him want her again because she was a different sort of woman, one he would admire for her drive and ambition and self possession, not just because of her exotic dress. And why couldn’t Harry keep out of her lovelife? His was hardly a model example. Camilla was welcome to him. He was a nuisance.

Harry nudged her gently with his elbow. “Look on the bright side. He might be jealous and he didn’t look the type to let some impoverished writer steal his girl.”

Grace smiled reluctantly. Could he be right? But she wasn’t Jeremy’s girl any more and Harry had probably just made sure she wouldn’t be.

“Are you impoverished?” she asked.

“Pretty much,” said Harry and raised his glass. “Cheers.”

Chapter Five

Time Line didn't win the fat check but it did win a prize for cover art and design which caused great celebrations at their table. The artist's name was Janis Reeves but she wasn't present. Clive accepted on her behalf.

Grace discovered she was inordinately disappointed that Harry's book didn't win. More disappointed than Harry who didn't seem too concerned and clapped enthusiastically as the winner stepped up to receive his award.

"Anna," asked Grace quietly when Harry was occupied talking to the person on his left. "Is Janis Reeves Harry's Janis?"

"Yes. She's a graphic designer, didn't you know? She did the cover art years ago when Harry first started the book and it was so good we kept it. She works for an advertising firm now. Very upmarket."

"I don't know anything much about Harry," admitted Grace. "He moved in next door a few weeks ago. I've met William though, briefly."

"He adores William," said Anna. "Quite frankly the boy would be better off living fulltime with Harry. Janis is too tied up in her career to give him much attention. I don't think she ever really wanted children. That was one of the problems, I think. Harry's basically an old fashioned, home loving man."

Grace nodded. Anna seemed to know a lot about Harry.

"Have you known him a long time?" she asked.

"Yes. Must be ten or even twelve years. I went to their wedding and I'm an honorary aunt." She laughed happily.

The formal part of the evening had finished. A man with a keyboard, energetic gyrations and a bank of speakers began pumping out far more sound than Grace thought possible or desirable given the source and the occasion. Several couples got up to dance. People left their places and table hopped, doing lots of cheek kissing, backslapping and congratulating or commiserating depending on circumstances. Their table got both. Grace sat and listened to Harry say the same thing politely over and over.

"Thanks, yes Janis's award is fantastic. She deserves it. I think *Time Line* should have won too but . . . there you go. Robert's book is excellent."

A black beclad bottom appeared next to Grace as its owner draped herself over Harry and kissed him vigorously leaving a scarlet slash on his cheek. Marking her territory. Branding her man.

"They don't know quality when they see it," she declared.

"Your book won, though," said Grace to the bare back and the covered backside. Camilla turned a blank face towards her, talon-like hand still resting on Harry's shoulder. She wore very thick make-up and glued on eyelashes. Grace smiled brightly. "Congratulations."

"Thanks. Would you mind, Grace, if I stole Harry away to dance?" An ingratiating and patently false smile.

"Of course not. I'm sure he'd love to, wouldn't you, darling? Just a moment." Grace pulled a tissue from her evening bag and wiped Harry's cheek ostentatiously. "There you are, sweetie."

Harry narrowed his eyes momentarily at Grace then stood up. He tossed his napkin on to the table. Camilla bared her teeth and led him away like a prize bull. Grace watched them reach the dance floor where Camilla wrapped her arms around Harry. There was a woman who didn't take no for an answer. Camilla wanted Harry and she wasn't about to admit defeat even previously in the face of a wife and now, in as far as she knew, a passionate, new love.

Grace scanned the room for Jeremy. He'd been sitting three tables away but she hadn't been able to decide if the thin faced, angular redhead next to him was his partner for the evening or not. She spotted him leaning over someone's chair and laughing. Networking. Jeremy knew exactly who to chat to and exactly for how long. Who to spend time with and who not to waste time with. She'd always loved his confidence and had been flattered and proud he'd chosen her.

Camilla still had Harry in her octopus embrace. He looked extremely uncomfortable and glanced across at Grace. She gave him a little wave and blew him a kiss. He scowled. Grace got up and headed for Jeremy. Camilla did it effortlessly, so could New Grace. Old Grace wouldn't have a hope. Old Grace had better keep quiet.

New Grace put a sway in her walk and held her head up high. She smiled serenely at the men who ogled her legs as she passed. That always happened when she wore this dress and in this company she certainly stood out. None of the women had worn anything exciting at all. Camilla's backless number was the most daring. Rather staid in the clothing area these business types. The winning authors had been predominantly male with a smattering of overwhelmed wives or girlfriends in department store evening gowns bought for the occasion.

The plump, red-faced man with Jeremy watched with an appreciative smile as Grace approached. Jeremy turned mid-sentence and his face registered initial annoyance followed by a hastily applied smile when he realized his companion was anxious to be introduced.

"Excuse me," Grace said politely.

"Not at all," cried the seated man and leapt to his feet. He swayed slightly and a wave of wine soaked breath enveloped her as he grabbed her hand in both of his. "And who are you, my gorgeous one?"

"Grace Richmond," said Jeremy. "Grace, this is," but he didn't get a chance to finish.

"James," cried her admirer.

"How do you do?" murmured Grace. "I'm sorry to interrupt but I was wondering . . ." she turned a brilliant Camilla style smile upon James, ". . . if I could possibly steal Jeremy from you to dance with me?"

"On one condition," he said and attempted a seductive expression which just made him look slightly cross eyed. "That you dance with me as well."

"No problem," said Jeremy. "Grace would love to, I'm sure."

He gave Grace a firm look which she assumed meant agree or else. James must be important to him. Grace returned the look with extra ice. She didn't want to dance with James, she doubted whether James would remain upright for much longer and his breath made her gag. But she wanted Jeremy. Grace wavered, made up her mind. No.

"I," she began but Jeremy put his arm around her and kissed her cheek softly.

"Thanks, Princess," he whispered in her ear. His old nickname for her. Princess Grace.

She changed her mind.

James dragged her on to the dance floor and his

hands immediately began pawing at her bottom. Grace held him away forcefully. "If you keep doing that I'll slap you."

"Oh, ho a feisty one. I like that," he said but he stopped the groping and adopted a more civilized clasp.

Camilla and Harry danced by. Harry lifted his eyebrow and grinned. Grace glowered. Camilla ran her hand up the back of Harry's neck and kept her eyes glued to his face. James lurched and stumbled and clutched at Grace to hold himself up.

"I've had enough, thank you." Grace walked off the dance floor straight across to where Jeremy sat watching with a satisfied look on his face. James trailed after her but got waylaid by an equally drunken group who insisted he join their table for a celebratory drink.

"Jeremy, dance with me," she ordered and took his hand.

"What did you say to him?" he asked. "I was getting on really well until you interrupted. The least you could do was be civil and dance with the man. You must have realized he was important to me."

"I want to dance with you, not that drunk," said Grace acerbically.

Jeremy gave her an astonished look. "That drunk happens to be an important client. He's worth a lot of money to us."

"Not to me he's not important," said Grace and was gratified to see the now stunned expression on his face. He must have expected an abject apology and capitulation, as usual. "He's disgusting," she added. "And I can't think why you would insist I dance with him. I'm not a piece of merchandise for barter in aid of your wheeling and dealing."

"What's come over you, Grace?" asked Jeremy. She sensed a change in his manner. Wary. He'd never been wary of her before. He took her for granted. This power felt good.

"I've decided to assert myself, that's all."

"Mmm, Princess," he murmured and she slipped into his familiar embrace. Jeremy held her close. She closed her eyes, remembered what it was about him that she'd loved. He kissed her cheek and buried his nose in her neck as they shuffled about virtually on the spot.

"That's my date you're pawing, buddy," said a voice.

Harry! Grace's eyes flew open. What was he doing? She'd made it clear she didn't want him to interfere where Jeremy was concerned. Hadn't she? Surely their little charade was over?

Jeremy regarded Harry with the disdainful look he used in court on recalcitrant witnesses. Grace had gone along once to watch him in action and been very impressed. Scorn dripped from every pore of his body.

"I don't think Grace was objecting. Perhaps she doesn't like her date," he said.

"Maybe but the fact remains she *is* my date and not yours and I would thank you to remember that fact."

"Harry!" said Grace fiercely, keeping her voice low. "I want to dance with Jeremy."

People were beginning to stare. And grin. Grace fixed Harry with a gaze that should have told him "go and sit down and be quiet" but obviously didn't because he said, "I want you to dance with me."

"Go ahead, Grace," said Jeremy, tightly. "We don't want a public brawl, do we? I'll call you tomorrow, Princess."

"Thank you," said Harry as Jeremy withdrew. "Now, there's a gentleman. I can see why you like him." He pulled Grace into his arms and held her firmly as she attempted to free herself.

"For heavens sake! What are you doing?" she hissed.

"It doesn't look good for our relationship to have you swooning in the arms of another man," he murmured as he swung her around a couple who were barely moving. "Jealousy is a potent force, remember . . . Princess."

"You're jealous?" asked Grace in surprise.

"Not me, your boyfriend," he said. "Didn't we agree to make him jealous?"

"Did we?"

"I thought the deal was, you protect me from Camilla, which by the way you failed dismally at, and I help make the man jealous."

"Oh," said Grace, deflated. But Jeremy *had* been dancing with her and he'd shown much greater interest in her and in a different way—until Harry interfered.

"But," she began, but Harry cut her off.

"Time to go?"

"If you like," she said, all bravado gone. "I'm your date. This is your night."

He gave her an odd look but led her off the dance floor and to their table where she collected her wrap. He draped it over her shoulders for her and they said good night to Anna and Michael who were sitting drinking coffee and giggling together. A happy married couple. It made Grace smile inside. At least some people managed it.

"Lovely to meet you, Grace," said Anna. "Hope we meet again." Michael saluted them.

Grace hoped she would see Anna again but the way Harry was acting at the moment she didn't have a clue whether he would ever invite her to anything again or not. He didn't appear to be angry. It was more like he was distant, preoccupied. Perhaps he was secretly disappointed about losing out on the prize and having his ex win instead. That would be enough to upset anyone. And he may have really needed the money.

They stood silently waiting for the elevator and stepped in together when it arrived. Harry pressed the button for the ground floor. Just as the doors began to close an arm reached in and forced them apart. Jeremy stepped through the gap.

"Oh!" His eyes darted from Harry to Grace, startled.

Grace smiled. So did Jeremy. Harry didn't smile. Harry said nothing. He put his arm around Grace's shoulders and turned her to face him. She looked up in surprise. He held her face gently with his other hand

and bent down to brush his lips very softly across hers. Then, when she didn't pull away because she was so stunned, he kissed her again. His arm pulled her close, wrapping her right around. Grace's eyes closed spontaneously, her lips parted of their own accord, her body sagged against his and her arms slid around his neck all by themselves. He tasted of coffee and just a hint of vanilla from dessert. She would taste of coffee and chocolate, from dessert. He was delicious and his mouth was exciting, his body was warm and firm against hers and she was pressed against his chest. Her legs felt weak and her whole body came alive, tingling and sparking and now both his arms were around her, holding her up because she could barely stand.

Jeremy cleared his throat.

Harry stopped kissing her. Grace swam to the surface in dismay. Her eyes fluttered open. His gray ones were smiling down into hers. He winked. He put her away from him and stuck his hands casually in his pockets.

He'd winked at her! After a kiss like that!

Jeremy looked as though he could cheerfully throttle them both. Grace could cheerfully throttle Harry. Grace resettled her shawl over her shoulders with her mind working overtime. Harry grinned at her again and she couldn't prevent a little smile creeping across her face. Two could play at this game. Whatever it was. Grace smiled deliberately at Jeremy.

Before she'd figured out her next move he'd snaked his arms around her, drawn her against his chest and planted his lips on hers. His kiss was the one she remembered from countless other times, expert and forceful. Jeremy in charge. The one she'd always enjoyed. Before.

But not now and certainly not in front of Harry.

The elevator doors opened. Grace extricated herself from his embrace and spun around. They had an audience of surprised faces. Strangers.

Harry had gone. Grace hurried out into the foyer of the hotel pushing past four sniggering, grinning people. Harry was striding towards the main entrance. Grace ran. Jeremy caught her after just a couple of steps.

"Grace, for heavens sake!" he said sharply. He grabbed her arm and she stopped. "Let the man go. You're making a spectacle of yourself."

"But he's gone!" she wailed, stricken.

"He's a loser," said Jeremy. "Anyway what did you expect? Come on, I'll take you home."

Grace stood uncertainly, gazing at the fast disappearing rear view of Harry's tuxedo. Jeremy pulled at her arm gently and she reluctantly followed him to the underground car park and his midnight blue something or other.

Harry's car wasn't in the garage when they pulled up outside Grace's house. Jeremy slipped his arm around Grace's shoulder and drew her towards him. She watched his familiar face swim closer and closed her eyes. His lips closed on hers. This is what she'd dreamt of, the whole *raison d'etre* for her personality makeover. Her life was back on track. Jeremy wanted her again. She was interesting and desirable. Not, as Harry had so viciously accused, an unattractive, uptight, spinster. Tears pricked at her lids. Why had he winked?

Jeremy drew away slightly. "What's up?" he asked softly. "Don't worry about that loser of an author, Princess." He kissed her again.

"I'm not," said Grace, pulling away indignantly.

"Good, he's not worth the paper he's written on." Jeremy laughed. He opened the door. "Come on. Let's continue this inside."

Grace opened her door and stepped out on to the footpath. Woof barked, deep and threatening from behind his high fence.

"Must be a nuisance, having that next door," commented Jeremy casually as he draped his arm over Grace's shoulder. His automatic key lock chirruped and Woof barked again.

"No, he's a lovely dog," said Grace. "He's no trouble at all."

They squeezed through the gate, side by side and Jeremy paused on the front step to kiss Grace again as she fumbled in her bag for the key.

"Jeremy," she said. "I can't . . ."

Car lights swept across them and Grace looked up into the glare of headlights as Harry turned into his driveway. His car door slammed and she heard his footsteps stomping on the cement path to his front door. Guilt flooded her whole body. Overwhelming, crippling guilt. Shame of the worst kind.

"I don't want you to come in," she said.

"Yes, you do," he wheedled and nuzzled her neck.

"No! I don't," cried Grace. "I'm too tired and we're playing out of town tomorrow night. It's too late and I have to get up early. Jeremy, I shouldn't have done that to Harry. He was my date."

"Don't worry about it. I'm here instead. He doesn't mean anything to you, does he?"

Grace firmed her mouth into a thin line. Harry didn't mean anything to her but that wasn't the point. Good manners were the point. Not hurting someone's feeling was the point. How could Harry kiss her like that? Were all his kisses like that?

"Does he?" asked Jeremy, pulling her into his arms.

"No." But Grace stood firm. "Good night, Jeremy. Thanks for driving me home."

"All right. Good night." Jeremy touched her cheek with the back of his hand. "Nice to see you," he said.

Grace nodded and watched him saunter down the path to his car. Woof barked as he passed and she heard him call, "Shut up, you mongrel." Then the car door slammed and with a throaty roar the midnight blue thing disappeared down Curston Road.

Grace stood in the darkness. The heavy perfume of roses from next door hung on the warm night air. Woof was quiet now but another dog barked a few streets away. An occasional car engine broke the silence. A light was on in Harry's side room.

Grace walked down her path and along the footpath to Harry's gate. She pushed it open, strode to his front door past the roses which were overpowering this close and knocked loudly. She heard muffled sounds then Harry stood before her in his socks and pants and open necked shirt. Warm yellow light glowed from the hallway behind him.

"Yes?" His partly shadowed face gave her no hints.

"I'm sorry." Grace stared at his shirt front.

"Good. You ought to be," he said. "Is that all?"

"Yes," said Grace. He began to close the door. "But you deserved it."

"Did I? Why?" He sounded only vaguely interested.

"Kissing me in front of Jeremy. Kissing me at all."

"It worked, didn't it?" His hand dropped to his side.

"It was totally unnecessary! He was already interested in me again," she cried, frustrated by his blandness.

"That's what you wanted then." Harry put his hand on the door again. "Good night."

Grace clenched her fists. There was more to say but she didn't know what it was and he wasn't helping. The door began swinging shut.

"Harry? Why did you kiss me? Really?"

"I told you . . ." He paused and for the first time she sensed he was engaged in their conversation. "And I just wanted to see what it was like." He cleared his throat.

"And did you?"

"Yes. And so did you."

Grace knew her face was slowly turning fiery red. She spun around and stalked away into the security of the dark.

"Don't worry. I won't do it again," he called.

"Good," yelled Grace. The door slammed behind her.

Harry stomped back to his study and turned off the light. He went to the kitchen and flung the back door open, surprising Woof who was lying on the mat and who leapt to his feet with a wagging tail. Harry sat on the back step.

He knew why he had kissed Grace. It was because tonight she was sexy and beautiful and she deserved better than that loser of a pawing lawyer. And he missed the softness and tenderness of a woman in his life, and he was disappointed about losing, and he was lonely.

He knew why he shouldn't have kissed her too. Because by day she was hard and brittle and exactly like Janis and the last thing he wanted was to be entangled with a woman like that. On any level. Ever. Lonely or not.

He rubbed Woof's soft head. And she didn't like dogs.

"But you like her, don't you?" he said and got up to go inside and try unsuccessfully to sleep.

* * *

Grace walked to Italian class on Monday. She wore a floppy straw hat and baggy linen shorts because it was getting hot now, nearly full summer. She wondered if Harry would go. If he had any sensitivity for her feelings he wouldn't, but he did, which indicated he didn't, and he sat across from her and ignored her and didn't offer her a ride home.

She walked home in the heat. Practice was her priority. The orchestra had a break of several days after their overnight concert in nearby Newcastle and Grace intended to make full use of the free time. Eric had continued North to visit his parents in Coff's Harbour, Marcel wandered in and out at all sorts of odd hours—she would be uninterrupted.

At four there came a tentative tap on the front door. Grace placed her violin and bow down carefully and frowned as she went to open it. William stood on the mat with a worried look on his hot, little face. His school bag rested against his ankles. She thought he might be about to cry.

"What's the matter, sweetie?" cried Grace.

"Dad's not home," he said and his lip trembled. "I can't get in."

"Is he expecting you? Come inside."

She led him through to the kitchen and sat him down on a chair with a glass of cold unadulterated apple juice. Thank goodness Marcel had restrained himself this time. William dumped his bag on the floor by his feet and took a deep drink.

"Is Harry expecting you?" she asked again. She couldn't imagine he would forget William was coming. "I thought you only stayed at weekends."

"He was supposed to pick me up."

"How did you get here?"

"By bus."

"Maybe his car broke down or he was held up. He's probably at school now, worrying where you are," she said, hoping Harry hadn't had an accident because that was the next logical assumption. "Can we call him or your mom?"

William shook his head. "Mom's gone away for a whole week, that's why I'm staying with Dad and he hasn't got a cellular phone."

"Well, no problem. You can stay here with me until he gets home," said Grace. "Do you need to use the bathroom or anything?" He looked as though he needed a bath. His face was hot and shiny with sweat and, she suspected, one or two grimy tears.

"Yes, please." He slid off the chair and followed Grace down the hall.

"I'll be in the living room," she said as he disappeared into the bathroom.

Where was Harry? Grace peered out the window. He'd be terribly worried to lose William. Frantic. He was upset enough when he lost Woof. But she mustn't panic William. Harry would be sure to come back home eventually and the child would be safe here. He'd come to her for help, she realized, trusting. She liked that.

"Is that a violin?" asked William.

"Yes."

"My friend Jordan plays the violin."

"Do you learn an instrument?" asked Grace.

William shook his head.

"Like to try?"

"No. I like cricket."

"Do you play? My brother plays for the local team." Grace led the way back to the kitchen. "Hungry?"

"Yes. I'm a fast bowler. Does he bat or bowl?"

Grace took out the cookie jar and they ate her home baked chocolate chip cookies and drank apple juice while she told William about her brother Ben's cricket career.

"I think I heard Dad's car," cried William suddenly and jumped up.

"Hope so." Grace followed him to the front door where he was wrestling with the lock.

"Dad!" William yelled and ran down the path. Woof bounded towards him.

"William, thank heavens! Where did you go?" shouted Harry from his driveway. "Why didn't you wait?"

"I did but you didn't come so I got on the bus."

"I did! I was a bit late, that's all. You should have waited. I didn't know where you were. Never, ever do that again."

Grace stood watching Harry hug William as if he'd never let him go. She smiled and a lump formed in her throat. Nothing compared to the love a parent has for a child. She walked slowly back down the path.

"Thanks, Grace." She turned. Harry was standing holding William's hand. He gestured vaguely with his free hand. "I don't know what . . . thank you."

Grace smiled. "That's okay. Any time."

"Thanks, Grace," said William. "Grace has home-made chocolate chip cookies," he said to Harry.

"Does she? Lucky you."

"My bag's in the kitchen."

"I'll get it," said Grace quickly. She pushed the door open to step inside. Woof ran after her. "No you don't," she said but he darted around her and in front of her legs as she moved and suddenly she was falling. Her arm flailed wildly as she grabbed for support but Woof had pushed the door wide and she missed it, landed heavily on her wrist. Something gave a sickening crack. A shaft of pain shot through her body. She cried out and heard Harry's voice call Woof through a mist of agony and rising nausea.

Chapter Six

Harry had his arm around her and lifted her gently to rest her back against the wall.

"Take Woof out," he said to William who grabbed Woof by the collar and pulled him away from Grace whose face he was trying to lick.

"My wrist," Grace said. Her voice hardly worked. She held her injured, screaming left wrist with her other hand. The skin was intact, there was no blood but it was agonizing.

"I think it's broken," said Harry. "We'd better get you to the hospital."

Grace heard him move through the house, the sound of a door closing, the back door. He reappeared beside her holding her handbag.

"Is this the right one?" he asked. "It was in the kitchen."

Grace tried to concentrate and focus on the bag. Brown leather, straps. She nodded.

"Are your keys in it?" She concentrated hard and nodded again.

Harry squatted and slipped his arm around her waist. He lifted her to her feet and she leaned against him as he walked her to his car. The pain in her wrist was unbearable, excruciating, every step jarred through her body and by the time Harry opened the car door and helped her in she was ready to collapse. She rested her head against the seat back and closed her eyes.

The back door opened and closed. William asked in a scared voice, "Grace? Are you all right?"

"I broke my wrist, I think," Grace managed to murmur.

"Woof tripped you," said William.

"Yes,"

"Does it hurt?"

"Lots."

"Dad's taking you to hospital, they'll fix it," he said. "Don't worry."

Grace smiled and her eyes filled with tears as his small hand patted her on the shoulder and she felt his warm breath on her cheek.

Harry got in beside her and started the engine. "Buckle up, William. I locked your house," he said to

Grace. "And Woof's in disgrace, the stupid, stupid animal. I'm so sorry, Grace."

The forty minute ride was the longest Grace had ever experienced. Never in all her life had she been in such excruciating pain. Stung by a bee at seven, falls from her bike, the occasional twisting cramp at period time, headaches, nothing had prepared her for this agony. She sat next to Harry oblivious to everything. He spoke occasionally to ask how she was and she managed to mutter something which seemed to satisfy him then retreated into her world of pain.

Next she was aware, Harry stopped the car right in front of the emergency entrance at the hospital and they were walking through the automatic doors to the emergency room, all white tiles and noise and bustling people and a sharp faced nurse asked her name and address and began filling out a form.

"We'll get that into a sling to give you some support," she said. "You need to keep it immobile. And no food or water while you wait."

She tied Grace up with expert fingers and then sat her down to wait amidst the ranks of other broken and miserable people. Harry disappeared saying he had to move the car or he'd get a ticket. William sat next to Grace.

"It's my fault," he said in a tiny voice.

Grace turned her head and looked down at his small body slumped in the blue plastic seat. He was wearing gray school shorts, his socks were crumpled around his ankles and one knee had a band aid on it. On his other side was a big man with a terrible, hacking cough and a rasping, wheezing pair of lungs.

"That's impossible and you mustn't think that, ever," said Grace.

"If I'd waited at school for Dad, Woof wouldn't have tripped you up," he insisted and his blue eyes had that worried sheen of tears again.

"Silly Woof might have tripped me up next time I saw him, anyway," returned Grace."You didn't tell him to. It's not your fault, William and I never for one minute thought it was. Neither will your Dad. I should have looked where I was going."

Grace took one of William's hands and squeezed it. "It was nice to have you come to visit," she said.

"Does it hurt?" he asked.

"A lot," she said.

Harry returned from the car park and found them sitting quietly side by side holding hands in the sea of sick people. He paused and watched in wonder for a moment. William barely knew Grace and here he was holding her hand. In fact, William had unhesitatingly turned to Grace when he was locked out and Grace had taken him in, cared for him and seen to it that he wasn't alarmed by the situation. Had fed him homemade chocolate chip cookies. And this is how she was repaid. Woof broke her arm.

On the drive to hospital Harry had expected a barrage of abuse and invective to start up. A woman with such a well developed sense of herself as Grace would be looking to lay the blame somewhere and on him via Woof was the obvious place. The Janises and the Graces of this world didn't believe in accidents just happening, they liked to find the root cause and let fly. There was always a culprit in any given situation.

And this meant Grace wouldn't be able to play her violin for months. Harry braced himself and went to stand before the pair.

William let go Grace's hand and got up. Harry sat down.

"All right?" he asked Grace. She was very pale and a light film of perspiration stood on her brow and upper lip. Without thinking, Harry pulled out his handkerchief and patted gently at her face.

She swivelled her eyes to his and her lips curved in a very faint smile.

"No," she murmured. "Stupid question."

"I'm sorry."

"So you keep saying," she said. Here it came. He knew she wouldn't be able to restrain herself and really she had every right to lay into him. Call him all sorts of names for not keeping his dog under control—the way she'd done last time when Woof had run away.

But she didn't. She closed her eyes and sat in silence. In too much pain, probably. Shock. Poor darling. The avalanche would come later.

"Would you like something to drink?" he asked.

"She's not allowed, Dad," piped up William.

"Oh, that's right," said Harry. "How about you?"

"Not if Grace can't," he said manfully.

Grace said, with her eyes still closed, "Go ahead William, if you like. I don't feel like eating, anyway. I think I'd be sick."

Harry pulled some money out of his pocket and sent William off to the snackbar visible further along the corridor towards the foyer. He took Grace's hand and folded it in both his. She opened her eyes and looked at him.

"You don't have to stay, Harry," she said. "I'll be here for ages."

"We'll stay," he said and thought she seemed pleased because she didn't insist they leave and she didn't move her hand.

"William thinks it's his fault."

"Do you?" Harry unconsciously tightened his grip on her fingers.

"No, of course not. I thought maybe you'd like to reassure him, too."

"Yes, I will. Thanks."

Someone called Grace's name. Harry stood up quickly and helped Grace to her feet.

"We'll wait here," he said. "They'll x-ray you after this."

He watched Grace walk away behind the nurse then sat back down to wait for William. He came back ten minutes later laden with two cans of soda and two large packets of potato chips. They slurped and crunched and waited and William fidgeted until Grace reappeared and told them she had to go to the x-ray department.

"Why don't you two go home?" she said. "I'll have to wait again down there and then wait for the results and then wait to have my arm put in a cast. It's going to take hours. Go home."

Harry looked at William and then at Grace. He should take William home. It was deadly dull for him and would get worse. William would need dinner and most likely had homework to do. Grace was right but could he walk out and leave her here? How would that look?

"You'd rather go home, wouldn't you?" Grace asked William.

He nodded. "Only if you'll be all right by yourself."

"I'm hardly by myself," said Grace. "And they've given me a painkiller."

"I'll take William home as long as you promise to phone as soon as you're finished. We'll come to pick you up." Harry bent his head to catch Grace's eye and make her see he was serious.

She gave him a cursory acknowledgment and said, "Okay I'd better go to x-ray now and get in the line."

"See you later." Harry leaned forward and kissed her on the cheek taking care not to touch the poor, damaged arm in the sling. Her skin felt cold and clammy. He wanted to hug her tight and make everything better because she seemed like a lost and lonesome child all of a sudden and his heart went out to her.

It seemed to Grace as though she had always been in the hospital and that she always would be, sitting waiting in different colored, uncomfortable, plastic chairs surrounded by people in various degrees of pain and suffering. The painkiller only dulled the razor sharp edge of the hacksaw at her wrist and for most of the time she sat with eyes closed trying not to move, trying not to think.

Eventually, maybe in the middle of the night—Grace had no idea because her watch had broken in the fall—it was over. They'd x-rayed, examined, declared there was no need for surgery involving pins and screws and plates but set her wrist at what seemed an unnatural angle and then immobilized it with a pink cast and a sling.

"Is someone waiting to take you home?" asked the discharge nurse while Grace signed various pieces of paper with her good right hand.

"I have to call," said Grace. "What's the time?"

"Ten." Almost the middle of the night. No wonder she was exhausted, she'd been here nearly five hours.

"I'll get a taxi." Far too late to ask Harry to pick her up. William would be asleep. Grace wiped the back of her hand across her brow, yawned and the nurse smiled one of the cheery, nurse type, sympathy smiles.

"Take those painkillers when you need to but don't overdo it. Try to get some sleep. The pain will ease in a day or two. There are phones over there and taxis are often outside at the taxi line."

Grace murmured her thanks and went to call Harry to tell him not to wait up. She searched awkwardly in her purse for coins and discovered that even the smallest, simplest things were going to be difficult for the next six weeks. Then she discovered she didn't have Harry's phone number. Then she decided she was too tired to bother going through directory assistance, she wanted to go home, so she climbed wearily into the next taxi in the line and was carried half asleep, to Curston Road.

No-one was at home. The house loomed dark and silent. Grace paid the taxi driver and went to tap on Harry's door. He flung it open and when he saw her, heaved a sigh of relief and hustled her inside.

"Thank heavens!" he cried. "I didn't know what could have happened. I imagined all sorts of things—surgery, amputation." He laughed but it was a tense sound. "Why didn't you call? I would have come straight back."

"I didn't have the number," said Grace. "I want to go home and go to bed, Harry. I only came to tell you I was home."

"Of course. You must be worn out. Is it still painful?"

"Not quite as bad but yes. I'm doped up to the eyeballs." Grace stepped back outside and turned to find Harry right behind her. "You don't need to come with me," she said but he followed her along the path between the roses.

"I'll help you get settled," he said. Grace was too tired and fuzzy in the head to object. "Are you allowed to eat yet?"

"I'm not hungry."

Harry put out his hand as they reached her doorstep. "Keys?"

Grace fumbled about in her bag and found them. They went inside. Harry switched on lights and closed the front door.

"I'm going straight to bed," said Grace.

"You'll need help undressing."

"I won't."

"You will," he said. "Don't argue."

Grace thought he might be right as she pictured taking off her sandals and shorts and trying to get her T-shirt over her head. She needed to wash and use the toilet but she wasn't going to let him help her do that.

She led the way to her bedroom. Harry closed the curtains and pulled back the bedcover. Grace sat on the bed and he knelt and unbuckled her sandals. She watched through a kind of haze. He seemed remote. Her arm hurt and the cast felt heavy and cumbersome. She couldn't summon the energy to stand up, let alone begin taking off her clothes or visiting the bathroom.

"I need to wash my feet," she said. "I hate to go to bed with dirty feet."

The whole idea of washing her feet took on overwhelming proportions and Grace felt tears beginning to slide down her cheeks. She sat and sobbed silently. Harry looked up quickly from where he knelt on the floor. In a moment he was sitting next to her and cuddling her the way she imagined he might cuddle and console William. She rested her head against his shoulder and cried and felt, in his arms as though she had indeed, come home.

Harry stroked and soothed until the barrage of tears slowed to an occasional sniff, then he said, "Come on. Into the bathroom and we'll get you cleaned up and into bed."

"I'm sorry," said Grace in a tiny voice but he said, "Ssh. It's delayed shock, Grace. I'm just amazed you didn't let go earlier. You're a brave girl."

Holding her, feeling her body nestling against him, comforting her, she was defenceless and soft and unbelievably desirable. Harry looked into her red and tearstained eyes and thought if she hadn't had her arm in a sling and been in such a state he'd kiss her again the way he had in the elevator.

Instead he guided her to the bathroom and sat her on the edge of the bath to wash her feet. He kept his attention focussed on the soap, the taps, the plug, the water temperature and the foot he was washing and tried not to let his mind stray to the bare legs touching his shoulder and arm as he stretched across her body. Or her right arm which rested lightly on his back for support.

"I feel like the Queen," said Grace and he smiled as he heard the little giggle.

"Foot washing is a talent few can claim," he said. "I practice on Woof now that William is too big."

He straightened up, unwilling to risk touching her any longer. She clung to him as she turned around awkwardly and lifted her legs over the side of the bath. He took the towel she indicated and dried her legs, rubbing vigorously and quickly so she wouldn't suspect or notice the effect she had on him.

"I think I can get undressed myself, Harry," she said. "Shouldn't you go back to William?" Her voice was brighter now but still a long way from the prickly Grace he knew.

"He's fast asleep," he said but thought it might be wiser to leave right now or he'd again be tempted to kiss her. Like that Friday kiss and the response that found its way interminably into his head.

"I can get Kirsty to help me tomorrow." Grace smiled. "Thanks."

"It's the least I can do," Harry said seriously. He moved toward the door. "I'll lock the front door on my way out. You get straight to bed."

"I will," said Grace.

Grace woke the next morning stiff and uncomfortable and in pain. Her right arm had gone to sleep because of the way she'd been forced to lie to give her left arm some relief. She sat up slowly and grimaced as the blood rushed with excruciating pins and needles into the arm. Now she had two incapacitated limbs.

She heard the bathroom door open and Marcel's unmistakable tread on the floor by her door.

"Marcel," she called. "Marcel?"

His shaggy head appeared round her door.

"Morning, Grace," he said. "Having a sleep-in?

You're usually up and at it by now. Oh no!" His eyes opened wide with surprise and he came further into the room to study her arm and the pink cast. "What happened?"

"I tripped over Woof and broke my wrist yesterday afternoon."

"Clumsy!"

"Yes," she said. Trust Marcel to sum things up succinctly. "Is Kirsty here?"

"Yeah, she's in the kitchen making tea."

"I need her to help me shower and get dressed."

"Okay. Does it hurt?"

"Yes."

"Okay." Marcel disappeared out the door and Grace heard him yelling to Kirsty as he went thumping down the hall.

She eased her legs out of bed and sat on the edge to get her bearings. The door flew open and Kirsty rushed in. Amidst exclamations and questions, helpful suggestions and a supportive pair of hands Grace managed a shower and a welcome change of clothes having slept in her T-shirt and underwear to avoid the struggle of taking them off.

She sat at the kitchen table while Marcel and Kirsty fussed and fed her toast and cups of tea.

"What a total bummer," said Marcel as he studied the cast. "Can I be the first to sign it?"

"Go ahead," said Grace and rolled her eyes at Kirsty who just grinned.

Marcel found a pen and drew a picture of a double bass surrounded by flowers and his name. He gave the pen to Kirsty and then went through to the living room and started practicing his bass.

"What are you going to do now?" asked Kirsty.

Grace looked at her blankly. "What do you mean?"

"You know, the new woman? You were going really well from what I hear and what you said about Jeremy at the dinner."

"Yes, Jeremy," said Grace and stopped. Jeremy hadn't entered her head beyond reporting to Kirsty on Saturday morning when they sat in the garden having breakfast in the shade and watched Marcel weeding his vegetables. Harry had entered her head. Harry strayed constantly into her head and roamed about in there as if he had taken up residence.

"Won't Jeremy like the cast?" prompted Kirsty.

"I don't know. Probably not his idea of a sophisticated woman." Grace paused. "He hasn't phoned. He said he'd call and he hasn't."

"Mmm. But he doesn't know you've broken your wrist."

"That means he doesn't want to get back together and was just taking advantage of the situation." A leopard can't change its spots. Jeremy would take his time as he always had.

"What about Harry?"

Grace's cheeks warmed uncomfortably as she remembered the Harry/Jeremy scenario in the elevator.

She hadn't told Kirsty every detail of the night's entertainment. Censorship had been heavy.

"Harry was very kind to me but his dog had just broken my arm so he really didn't have much choice, did he?"

"Harry *is* very kind, Grace," said Kirsty.

"In patches. We tend to rub each other up the wrong way so the less we have to do with each other the better. Especially now."

Kirsty got up and cleared the table.

"William is a lovely little boy," said Grace. "He was terribly upset, thought it was his fault but it wasn't. It wasn't anybody's fault."

"That sounds like the old Grace," teased Kirsty. She filled the sink with water and detergent and began to wash the breakfast dishes.

"Well it wasn't anyone's fault," cried Grace. "If it was anyone's it was mine. I should have been more careful."

"Grace!" cried Kirsty, laughing out loud. "Stop it. The dog shouldn't have been allowed to run into the house. Your house, by the way, not his. The shock has made you have a relapse. Remember! Be strong, be determined, don't be so amenable."

"It hasn't done me much good, has it? My new assertiveness," said Grace. "I've offended and upset the new neighbour, who thinks I hate animals and dogs in particular, annoyed the girl at the supermarket, irritated a complete stranger, annoyed Jeremy by being rude to his business associate, been catty towards a well-known children's author, upset Eric and Marcel and Edward at work and broken my wrist. And I hate wearing those short, tight skirts."

Kirsty waved the sponge at Grace. Suds and water flew about. "Look!" she cried. "Lots of positives have come out of this."

Grace waited. Kirsty frowned. Her face brightened.

"You can speak Italian."

"*Si*."

"You've made Eric and Marcel more useful in the kitchen and Marcel has managed to expand his curry repertoire and that *has* to be a good thing."

"True."

"From what you told me that guy at the dinner was so drunk he was nearly falling over and only wanted to grope you anyway and that author woman was a predator who was after your date."

"True."

"Well?"

"Well what?"

"You've made changes, Grace. And you're working towards moving up in the orchestra. You'd never even mentioned doing that before. Marcel says your playing has improved out of sight."

"Kirsty!" Grace gripped the table with her free hand. Her eyes filled with tears and Kirsty darted forward in alarm.

"What is it?"

"I can't play," Grace wailed. "It just hit me then. Right then when you mentioned the orchestra. I can't play at all. I can't do the audition, I can't go to work. The doctor said I'd have this cast for at least six weeks and then if the bones haven't healed properly I'll have it on for longer. He said sometimes this sort of break takes much longer—months. I never even thought . . . why didn't I realize . . . and then I'll need physical therapy to strengthen it and make it flexible. He asked me what I did and I told him but it just didn't register. Why didn't it, it's so obvious?"

"You were in shock," said Kirsty. "And in too much pain to think straight." She pulled a second chair around and sat on it to face Grace who stared at her in horror.

"What if I never play again? What will I do? I can't do anything else. I don't want to do anything else!"

Kirsty gripped Grace's good hand tightly. "Don't think like that. You'll have to wait and see. They'll give you sick leave, won't they?"

Grace nodded. "But I'll miss the chance at the second desk position."

"Yes but there'll be other opportunities."

Someone knocked on the door and Grace heard Marcel go to open it. Harry. She recognized his voice. Footsteps sounded down the hallway then Harry stuck his head around the door. He smiled when he saw Kirsty. Marcel's bass started up again in the other room.

"Hi Harry," said Kirsty. "I'd better get going. Bye

Grace." She leaned down and kissed Grace's cheek. "Take care. Chin up. I'll be back later and if you like I'll stay for a few days to give you a hand."

"Thanks, Kirsty, That'd be wonderful."

Harry smiled at Kirsty as she left then sat down in the chair she'd vacated, close to Grace. She looked better this morning, more color in her cheeks and had obviously showered and changed her clothes with Kirsty's help. He wished she'd have let him help last night but of course he couldn't expect that. He couldn't expect anything from her. It was enough to be allowed into the house. He'd never seen her in baggy purple harem pants before with her hair all loose and soft around her face. He wanted to kiss her.

"I can't play," said Grace before he could ask how she was feeling. "I may not be able to play the violin ever again. Sometimes injuries like this don't heal properly." Her voice rose a little higher and got a notch louder with each sentence.

Harry gulped and swallowed. This was what he'd been dreading. What she had just said had occurred to him almost immediately last night but she must have been in too much pain and shock to think of the consequences.

"I know," he said and kept his voice deliberately low and calm.

"What am I going to do?" she cried, her face contorting in anguish. "How am I going to earn a living?"

"Grace, it may not come to that," he said. "Wait and see."

"That's easy for you to say," she said. "You can type with one finger if you need to. I can't play with one hand. You've got a house of your own. I'm paying rent. What happens when I can't afford it?"

She was nearly shouting at him now. He mustn't shout back.

"Grace, calm down," said Harry. "It won't come to that and if it does, if you do get kicked out on your backside, which I doubt . . ." He laughed to show her how ridiculous he thought the scenario, ". . . well in that case you can live with me."

"And Woof, I suppose," she said with a curl of her lip.

Harry clamped his mouth shut and leaned back in the chair. He breathed deeply and said, "There's nothing I can say beyond apologizing, Grace."

"No." Grace stood up and Harry stood as well.

"I'd better go," he said. Gone was the soft and helpless woman of yesterday, the one who sobbed in his arms and let him hold her and comfort her and who rested her head on his shoulder like a child. The one he could fall in love with as easy as falling over. Prickly and angry Grace was back with a vengeance and the worst part was, she had every right to be worried and upset about her future and it was his fault.

"I think it's probably best if you don't come over for a while Harry," said Grace. "I can't . . . I don't want to see you. And keep the dog locked up." Her voice was distant and cold.

"Sure," he said and made his escape before things

got even more unpleasant and she was tempted to make statements about him that he really didn't want to hear. He walked down his front path between the roses and stopped, picking off the odd deadhead.

He'd have to make sure William kept out of her way as well. He certainly didn't want to expose him to any of her invective. Yesterday she'd insisted William wasn't to blame but today in the cold light of reality might be a different matter. What an unholy mess! Darn Woof with his big clumsy body and his eagerness to investigate her house.

Harry raised his face to the sun shining hotly and enthusiastically down from a cloudless sky. He closed his eyes and groaned aloud. All he wanted was a quiet life, with his son and his dog and his writing. He opened his eyes and stared at the house. It had seemed perfect that day months ago when he and William had piled out of the car and made their initial examination from the footpath.

They hadn't checked out the neighbors. Big mistake. Would meeting Grace first have put them off buying the place? Not William. And Marcel and Eric were no problem. He could see himself becoming good friends with Marcel. They had the same taste in music and books. Grace hadn't heard of him let alone read one of his novels.

But she was a beautiful and attractive woman and he couldn't deny the desire he felt for her at the oddest moments. Right from the instant he'd laid eyes on her.

She was attracted to him too, he knew that for a fact. She wouldn't have kissed him that way if she wasn't. What an impossible and hopeless situation! He could never live with a volatile, emotionally unstable woman like that. Not only was she as ambitious and career minded as Janis, she veered wildly between soft and feminine and hard and aggressive. He never knew which Grace he was dealing with until she either reared up and snapped his head off or collapsed in his arms. And she displayed those weird flashes of unselfish kindness and empathy. Plus she was a talented, artistic woman, She'd be perfect if it wasn't for . . . Harry flung the deadheads on to the garden bed. He was going round in circles. Hopeless!

He should get to work. Having William stay for the week added disruptions to his routine and he wanted to make certain he wasn't late for the three o'clock pick up. He'd need to organize a sitter for the Thursday night class, too. It was lucky his other lectures were finished for the semester. Study time leading up to exams was in progress which meant he'd have piles of papers to mark soon. Harry pushed the front door open and headed for his study.

As soon as Harry left, Grace charged into the living room and picked up the phone, ignoring Marcel who was plunking away on his bass in the corner with his eyes closed. Her violin sat in its case on the table where she'd left it and she stared at it as she dialled the number for the orchestral manager. She came straight to the point.

"Hello, Ian, it's Grace Richmond. I've broken my wrist." She waited through the exclamations of dismay and regret and all the rest of it and asked, "What will happen?"

"You'll take sick leave, of course and we'll employ a substitute until you're ready to come back."

"So you'll hold my position?" she asked.

"Yes. It's such a shame, Grace."

"Tell me about it," she said and after a few more consoling words from Ian she hung up, marginally reassured about her immediate financial future.

"Go with the flow, Grace. Be cool," said Marcel still with his eyes closed and still playing. "Let your spirit shine through." He plucked an expressive chord and let the sound ring.

"I'm trying," Grace said through clenched teeth.

Later that afternoon she took some Italian homework out into the garden, sat under a tree on the grass and tried to learn various phrases. Brandy the cat came and rubbed against her. Brandy minded her own business and kept to herself.

"*Come stai*?" she asked. Brandy purred. She'd have to learn to say, "My arm is broken" to appease Roberto. And "Yes, I am in pain."

Car doors slammed from next door. She heard William's voice as he chattered to Harry and Harry's lower pitched responses but couldn't distinguish words. She shut her Italian book and lay flat out on the grass staring up at the leaves gently stirring on the tree above her. Her arm hurt, ached with an intense throbbing pain. The painkiller she took this morning must be wearing off.

What would she do with herself for the next six weeks? Study Italian? Read? Maybe even borrow one of Harry's books from Marcel, she'd be so bored. Everything would be difficult. Washing, dressing, cooking, cleaning, sleeping . . .

She could go to the movies during the day, go for walks, visit art galleries and museums. Treat it like a vacation. But she didn't want to take a vacation! She'd been enjoying practicing, had been getting all fired up with the idea of auditioning and beating Edward into that second desk position. Grace smiled to herself. Kirsty was right, she had changed. That was definitely a New Grace thought.

What about Harry? She'd been rude to him. His face had displayed just how rude. Harry. She didn't really not want to see him ever again. Old Grace making a reappearance.

A door slammed next door and she heard William call to Woof and the scuffle of feet as they ran around the yard. She closed her eyes.

"Grace?"

She sat up. William's head was just visible over the fence. He must be standing on something. Grace pushed herself up with difficulty, awkward to stand up with only one arm available for leverage. She walked across to him.

"Hello."

"Are you better today?"

"A bit, thank you. I don't feel sick and it doesn't hurt quite so much now I've got the sling to support it."

"Dad said I wasn't to bother you," he said.

"You're not bothering me. What are you standing on?"

"A garden chair."

"Well, be careful, you don't want to end up like me."

"I won't. Can I come to visit you?"

"Sure. I'm getting bored already because I can't play my violin. I was sitting here wondering how I was going to amuse myself for the next six weeks."

"Maybe I can come on Thursday when Dad goes to his class."

"If you like," said Grace. How would Harry react to that idea? "Your dad will have to decide. He might have other plans."

"He doesn't, he told me he doesn't know yet who'll watch me."

"I could come to your house," she said.

"Great!" cried William. "We can play Monopoly."

"William!" came Harry's voice from the back door. "I told you not to bother Grace. Sorry." His voice was stern. Maybe he shared her hastily spoken opinion that it was best they kept away from each other.

"Grace doesn't mind," replied William. "She's going

to play Monopoly with me when you go to your class on Thursday."

Harry stared at Grace across the width of the garden. Even from that distance she could see the look of displeasure on his face

"I don't think that's a very good idea," he said.

Chapter Seven

"Why not?" cried William in dismay.

"Come inside, William." Harry's voice was sharper than Grace had ever heard it. "Don't argue."

"Bye, Grace."

William threw Grace a miserable glance and disappeared. Grace turned and went to sit under the tree again. That was that. Now she knew how Harry felt. He didn't trust her with his son. The crazy woman from next door.

Saying she didn't want to see Harry didn't mean she included William. She'd have to make that quite clear, otherwise William would get the impression she blamed him for the accident. He'd be getting an odd impression already the way Harry had snapped at him just now. Grace plucked a handful of grass and rubbed it between her fingers. She'd have to go and get it straightened out. See Harry for the good of William. She clambered to her feet again. This sling made her lopsided and awkward.

Grace knocked on Harry's door. She heard the scuffle of paws and Harry's voice saying "Stay!" The noises stopped abruptly. The door opened. Harry glared at her and Grace nearly turned and ran. He towered over her standing on the little porch while he stood a step higher. Woof panted eagerly and thumped his tail on the floor. She glimpsed William peering interestedly from further down the hallway.

"Go outside, William," said Harry over his shoulder. "And take Woof." He waited until they'd gone then turned to Grace. "Yes?"

"When I said I didn't want to see you I didn't include William," she blurted.

"Oh."

"I don't want him to think I blame him for this." She lifted her slinged arm a fraction and winced as the angle sent a spasm through her shoulder. "And he might if you won't let him see me. He might think it's me who doesn't want to see him and it's not. It's you."

"Is it?" His eyes were on her face. Cool, blank.

"Isn't it?" she challenged.

"It was a natural assumption and I have to protect him."

"From me?" Grace cried.

"You made your opinion of me very clear and I don't want any of that to spill over to my son."

"You must have a very low opinion of me," said Grace, breathing hard.

"I don't know what to think of you. You change from minute to minute. It's very confusing and it's not something I want to expose William to."

"William and I get along very well. Why don't you ask him if he's confused about me?" demanded Grace. "He suggested I watch him on Thursday. He asked me!"

Harry shrugged and shook his head.

"If you're so worried I'll corrupt him, bring him over to my house and there'll be plenty of people to keep an eye on him. Unless you think Marcel and Kirsty and Eric are bad influences as well."

Grace stared at Harry until he dropped his gaze.

"All right. I'll bring him over on Thursday at about six thirty. Thank you." It sounded to Grace as though he was having a confession wrung out of him by the Inquisition. "I get home around ten."

"Fine. We'll give him dinner. Good bye." Grace turned and stomped down the path straight past the roses this time.

"Good bye." She heard the click of the latch as he shut the door. That look on his face when he'd talked about protecting William hurt almost as much as her arm. Did he think she wouldn't care for the boy? Add child neglect to the list of things Harry thought she was capable of.

William arrived clutching his Monopoly box and with a grin from ear to ear on Thursday evening. Early, just after six o'clock.

Eric opened the door and from the kitchen Grace could hear Harry apologizing for the time and how William couldn't wait a moment longer to come over.

"Doesn't matter," said Eric. "We're only watching Kirsty and Marcel prepare dinner."

"Smells pretty good," said Harry and then all three appeared in the kitchen.

William stood shyly, smiling at Grace and casting awestruck glances at Marcel who had a sleeveless T-shirt on and his tattoos in full view. Grace realized he hadn't met Marcel before and the experience for an eight year old could be similar to coming face to face with a yeti.

"Hello, William," she said. "This is Kirsty and that's Marcel. It's their turn to cook tonight. Marcel usually only cooks curry but we're getting sick of that so Kirsty is making lasagne. Do you like lasagne?"

The worried look which had passed across William's face at the mention of curry, faded and the grin reappeared as he nodded enthusiastically.

"And salad from my garden," added Marcel. "Want a drink, Harry."

"No, no I've got to go and teach," said Harry.

"Thank you, everyone, for looking after William. I'll be back around ten." He glanced at Grace and looked away again.

"How's your arm?" asked William, sitting down next to her and plonking the Monopoly box on the table.

"Doesn't hurt so much, now," Grace said, conscious of Harry watching them together. What did he think she was going to do? Pinch him on the leg under cover of the table? "Like to sign my cast?" She extended her arm towards him, carefully, as some movements squeezed and hurt the strained muscles and tendons in her shoulder.

"Can I?"

"Of course."

"Can Dad sign, too?" asked William and turned around on his chair to look at Harry. "Look, Dad. Look what Marcel drew."

Harry stepped closer and peered over William's shoulder at Grace's cast sporting the drawing of the double bass.

"Very nice," he murmured.

"Here you go," said Kirsty and handed William a felt tipped pen.

"What will I write?" he asked. "I'm not a very good drawer."

"Just write your name," suggested Grace.

William leant over her arm and painstakingly wrote his name and then drew a ball and a cricket bat.

"Excellent," said Grace admiring his lopsided artwork. "I like cricket."

"I know," said William.

"Like to go out in the yard and hit a few balls around?" asked Eric who had been leaning in the doorway watching.

William sprang off the chair and they were gone with the back door banging behind them.

"Go on," said Kirsty in a resigned voice to Marcel who was staring out the window longingly. "I'll clean up and be with you in a sec."

"Luv ya," said Marcel and kissed her. Kirsty patted him on the behind as he went and they heard him saying, "Watch out, men. Here comes the demon bowler," as he opened the screen door.

"Bye William," said Harry into the quiet of the kitchen and Kirsty laughed.

"Don't worry about him, Harry. Those two are big kids themselves."

She bent down and slid the lasagne dish into the oven. "That's that. See you later, Harry. I'm a demon batter myself."

"Thanks Kirsty," said Harry.

She strode purposefully out the door to the yard where cries and shouts of laughter indicated a riotous game was already in progress.

Silence. Grace sat unmoving at the table and stared at her cast with its signatures and decorations. Harry stood, uncomfortable and unsure of what to say. William had rushed outside with nary a backward glance. How could he have worried that he wouldn't be safe in Grace's house? With Grace. William couldn't wait to come over and Woof had already invited himself twice with disastrous results both times. They'd have both been on Grace's doorstep at four if Harry hadn't been firm with William and left Woof behind. Now, with a game going he'd be lucky to get his boy home at all.

Grace stood up. "I'll show you out."

He owed her another apology. He insulted her continuously and gratuitously. He'd accused her of everything from dog-hating to frigidity and insanity. She must detest him and with very good cause.

"Grace," he said as they went down the hall to the front door. "I'm sorry for insulting you the other day. I'm sorry for just about everything I've ever said to you. I'm sorry." He stopped as Grace faced him with her hand on the door latch. Her face had a look of sphinx-like impenetrability and her eyes were like flints.

"So you darn well should be," she said and opened the door. "Just in case you still have qualms about William's well-being, be assured he's in good hands. You saw for yourself."

Harry nodded and started to apologize again. Grace cut him off mid sentence.

"Is there a phone number where we can reach you? In case something happens, like he contracts leprosy or the house burns down?"

Harry pulled a card out of his wallet and scribbled a number on it. "That's the University switchboard."

Grace didn't even glance at it but she stepped aside and made it very clear he should leave.

He went.

On the way to his class and for most of the two hours of its duration, Harry pondered the enigma that was Grace. She was one hard woman, he decided but she wasn't going to take out her dislike of him on William. He believed her when she said that and anyway the others were there to dilute any bad feelings that might surface. And William patently adored her.

The image of Grace and William sitting holding hands in the hospital waiting area flashed through his head. Anyone would have taken them for mother and son. Except for the coloring. Grace's hair was dark with lustrous thick waves, while William had inherited Janis's sandy blondness and blue eyes.

He remembered with a cringemaking shaft of embarrassment what he'd shouted at her on her doorstep when Woof went missing. Something about making sure she never had children because she was so self obsessed.

The best he could do would be keep right out her way until she forgot, or at least until the memory wasn't so sharp and tangled up with all the other awful things he'd said to her. He had a feeling that would be a very long time if, as he suspected, she was from the same mould as Janis. Janis remembered everything and used her weapons skillfully and with great attention to detail, attributes that served her well in her profession but grated unbearably in a marriage. Forgiving and forgetting were not words in her vocabulary.

Would they be in Grace's? Not for at least six weeks while her broken wrist healed.

Harry sighed. And he thought he might be in love with the woman. He dismissed the notion from his head along with his class and headed for home. William would be tired and cranky tomorrow and would have to be dynamited out of his bed for school but the mere mention of someone taking him home and putting him to bed at nine had been met with such a howl of protest, Harry gave up.

Eric opened the door again and Harry followed him to the living room where the Monopoly board was spread on the coffee table and his son, Grace and Kirsty sprawled on the floor. The remains of a fruit cake sat on a plate nearby.

"William's a terrible cheat," said Eric as they went in.

"I am not!" cried William while Kirsty and Grace protested vigorously.

"Eric's just a poor loser," said Kirsty. "William's got the makings of a property tycoon."

Harry looked at William's shining, happy face and said, "I know, he always beats me."

"Dad's hopeless," said William. "He never remembers what he owns and forgets to collect the rent. Same as Grace."

"I just let you win," said Grace and smiled at William who scoffed loudly.

"Come on William. It's late," said Harry firmly. "Pack up the game, please."

"Can I come next week?"

"You'll be with your mom next week," Harry reminded him.

"Next weekend then," pleaded William. "You can go out somewhere and I can visit Grace and everyone."

Grace smiled and clambered to her feet with a helping hand from Kirsty who said, "Marcel and I are going to be away for the next month. We've got a tour coming up with the band."

William's face fell.

"And the orchestra has concerts for the next few weekends," said Eric. "But we can always play soccer in the day.'

"Great!" cried William. "And Grace needs company, don't you Grace? You'll be lonely with them all away."

Grace nodded. "I'd love you to visit, William but only if your dad agrees. He might like to see you as well, you know." She gave Harry a look he couldn't decipher but which confirmed his opinion that she was a woman who wouldn't forget in a hurry.

"We can all do something together," stated William cheerfully. "Can't we Dad?"

"Time for bed," said Harry. "Move it, mister!" He didn't dare glance at Grace to see her reaction to that suggestion but it was one he certainly wouldn't be acting upon.

* * *

Predictably, Grace's cast caused a stir in Italian class on Monday. Roberto fell over himself pulling out a chair for her and the others exclaimed and sympathized. Roberto then took charge and began giving them a blow by blow account of how he'd broken his arm at the age of thirteen by falling off his bicycle into a compost heap.

Harry wasn't there that morning and neither was Myra. Grace didn't go into too much detail about her fall.

"I tripped over going in the front door," she said. "Fell on my wrist."

Franco detoured into a vocabulary list of medical ailments and pain and they learnt how to tell each other they were sea-sick or needed a doctor to examine a swollen toe.

Time began to drag heavily for Grace. She worked out the practicalities of washing and dressing and on Tuesday afternoon managed to organize dinner one handed. At least it was her left arm out of action and she was able to wield a knife accurately in the kitchen and do things like sign her name properly when necessary and write Italian in class and for homework. But she couldn't do the one thing she really wanted. Practice the violin.

Grace went with Eric to a rehearsal and came home with more signatures on her cast and a pall of depression. She felt like an outsider all of a sudden, sitting listening, unable to join in. Edward commiserated and introduced her to her substitute, a serious young Chinese man named Vinnie who assured her how honored he was to take her place. Edward told her Vinnie was auditioning as well for the second desk spot and she smiled and wished him luck.

"I won't go in with you again, Eric," she said on the way home.

"Too depressing?" he asked and she nodded and felt tears pushing against her lids.

She swallowed hard and stared out the window away from him. Edward had told her how sorry he was but she had the distinct impression he was glad as well. He thought she was a threat to his ambition, a force to be reckoned with and never before had she got that feeling from anybody. Her strategy for New Grace had been working and now she was directionless again. Jeremy hadn't even called.

Perhaps she should call and tell him what had happened? Was that Old Grace or New Grace thinking? Grace sighed. It was all becoming too complicated. Where did she go from here? Neither Grace had reckoned with not being able to play the violin and work, at least in the short term. She wasn't ready to give it away just yet. There was nothing to take its place. She couldn't do anything else.

Eric reached out and patted her knee.

"Cheer up, love," he said. "You'll be playing again in no time."

"What if I can't, Eric?" she wailed as the tears broke

through. "What if my wrist doesn't heal properly? What do I do then?"

"Teach?" he suggested. "You'd be good at that. You could teach theory as well as violin."

Grace sniffed and groped for a tissue. He was right, she could do that. She'd never taught but plenty of players did, fitting students in around their orchestral schedules.

"I suppose," she said. "But could I earn enough to live off? Our rent's pretty steep and would you mind students coming into the house and listening to the racket they'd make? Imagine what Woof would do."

"He'd go hoarse," agreed Eric. "And Harry wouldn't be able to work."

"Yes, well, I don't care about that!"

"Grace, you don't blame poor Harry for your accident do you?"

"Whose fault was it then?" she cried. "Mine? Woof shouldn't have run into my house. He should've been on a leash."

"These things happen," said Eric mildly.

"Why do they happen to me?"

"Marcel thinks it's bad karma," said Eric. "Since you decided to change and be more aggressive you've upset the natural balance. Your yin is out of whack with your yang."

"What?"

"Something like that. Ask him."

Grace did, just before Marcel and Kirsty left in his loaded up car for their road trip with the band.

"It's not your natural way, Grace. You're going against the Tao," explained Marcel. "Everything affects everything else," he explained. "Every action you take has repercussions and you're taking actions which are causing cosmic upsets because they go against what is your natural path."

"Oh," said Grace. "What should I do?"

"Let your true spirit shine, Grace," he said. "The Tao will take care of everything else. Before, you thought you were too yin, then you became too yang as a counter to it. The pendulum swung too far. Balance your yin and yang. Let it flow."

"Thanks, Marcel," she replied, not really any the wiser but with a vague idea of what he meant. Maybe that's why being New Grace had been such a strain.

"Don't forget to water the garden," he said. "Be nice to Harry."

He gripped her in a big, fierce, bear hug and then passed her over to Kirsty to be kissed. They piled into his station wagon and Grace stood with Eric waving until they disappeared around the corner.

All right! Let her true spirit shine. She'd be nice to Harry if Harry was nice to her, something he seemed incapable of.

Jeremy called the next afternoon, Friday. Eric was out, Grace had just come in from a walk to the shops. She dumped the bag on the table and dashed for the phone.

"Hello Princess."

"Jeremy!"

"Why so surprised? I said I'd call, didn't I?"

"Yes, but . . ." She thought he'd done his usual trick of waiting to see if she'd call him, letting her call him. In actual fact she'd forgotten about him, she realized with a shock of surprise. The whole notion of winning him back by making herself irresistible and then ditching him in revenge seemed a total waste of time and effort. She couldn't be bothered. Was that New Grace asserting herself or Old Grace being typically undemanding?

"I know, I've been flat out here, didn't have a moment to take a breath. Do you want to go out for dinner tonight? There's a new place in Glebe that's supposed to be all the rage."

"Lovely, thank you," she said. It occurred to her briefly to complain that he'd left it very late to ask, as if he'd expected her to be panting with eagerness for him to call and that she'd drop everything at a moment's notice to go out with him. But Grace really didn't care and it would be lovely. An emotionally untaxing evening with a sophisticated man she liked and who knew how to give a woman a pleasurable evening out. And he wouldn't expect anything else because of her cast so that wouldn't be a problem at the end of the night. Jeremy didn't like awkwardness in any way, shape or form. Grace smiled as Jeremy told her when he would pick her up and she disconnected with a more cheerful air than she had had for over a week.

Eric had to help Grace button her skirt that evening. She'd chosen New Grace. Slimfitting burgundy skirt with matching jacket draped over her arm, a sleeveless black blouse, white sling supporting pink cast. Elegant gold chain and gold hoop earrings. Her hair had proved impossible to pin up one handed and with Kirsty away, so it had reverted to Old Grace curls and waves. A nice balance of Old and New Grace. Perhaps that's what Marcel meant.

"What did he say when you told him about your arm?" Eric asked.

"I didn't. It'll be a little surprise."

"I bet," he said and laughed.

Jeremy gaped when Grace opened the door to his peremptory knock.

"Still haven't fixed the bell," he was saying as she stepped into full view from behind the opening door.

"Hi Jeremy. No, not yet," said Grace airily. "Come in."

"What happened to you?" he asked when he'd recovered enough to close his mouth.

"I fell and broke my wrist."

"Good grief! Does it hurt?"

"Not much now but it did when it happened."

"Are you . . . I mean . . . can you?"

"What?"

"Do you want to go out to eat?"

"Of course! I'm dying to try this trendy new place," she said.

"Oh all right, fine. Let's go."

She could tell by the set of his mouth that a date with a woman wielding a pink cast on her arm was not his idea of a sophisticated, trendsetting evening. He held the door open and assisted her into the sporty blue machine. Grace managed to pull her seat belt across and buckle it up all by herself. Jeremy strode around and got in beside her. He started the engine and gunned the accelerator watching the rev meter critically.

"Think she needs a tune up," he murmured.

"Sounds like it to me," agreed Grace.

Jeremy shot her a suspicious look but she smiled and said, "It's a lovely car, this one," which diverted his attention sufficiently for a few minutes while he explained about the acceleration speed from zero to a hundred and the extra power to be gained from the drive shaft configuration. Or something similar. Grace understood more Italian then the English he was speaking.

"There's your neighbor and his unruly animal," said Jeremy capturing her attention. "Who's the kid?"

"That's William, his son," said Grace and waved as they shot past. She saw William's surprised face as he tried to figure out who was waving and then Harry said something and she glimpsed him wave wildly as they rounded a corner.

"Does he bother you at all?"

"Bother me?" asked Grace. Did Harry bother her? Yes, a lot and in many different ways. "Not recently, no. Why?"

"I don't like the look of him," said Jeremy. "I see a

lot of shifty types in my work and that guy . . . there's something about him."

"That's ridiculous!" cried Grace, coming to Harry's defense without quite knowing why. "He's not a criminal. Just because he doesn't much care about clothes and appearances doesn't mean he's shifty. He's an author, an artist."

"A parasite on society." He laughed as he said it and she knew he was deliberately overstating his opinion because he didn't like Harry. But it still made her mad.

"Jeremy, he's a lecturer at the University. Do you think I'm a parasite on society?"

'No, because you work. Anyone can say they're an author and apply for grants and get them and do no work at all."

"Harry is a published and successful author. I can't believe you're saying those things. You're an awful snob, you know that Jeremy?"

"Grace, what's come over you?" cried Jeremy. "This isn't like you at all."

"It is me, Jeremy, I just haven't said what I really thought before, that's all. You do it all the time. Why can't I?" she replied angrily. Why on earth had she accepted his invitation? Perhaps she should ask him to take her home although the way things were shaping up he might suggest it himself.

Jeremy surprised her by giving a shout of laughter. "You're absolutely right! You know, I like this side of you, Grace. Bit more pepper, not so bland."

"Do you?"

"Mm-mm," he said and slid his hand on to her knee.

Grace removed it and crossed her legs.

"I get the message, Princess." Jeremy sighed.

"Sorry."

He looked at her through narrowed eyes for a moment and then returned his gaze to the traffic.

"Why don't I believe you really mean that?" he asked.

The trendy new restaurant was noisy and crowded. Jeremy waved to several people he knew as they waited to be seated and Grace looked around wondering if any of her musician friends were trendy and up-to-date. Apparently not. She didn't recognize a soul.

Over drinks and a basket of herb and garlic bread which arrived very quickly they studied the menu. Grace chose a pasta dish which she knew would only require a fork while Jeremy eventually and after much discussion with the waitress, decided on an appetizer as well as a main course. They ordered and sat back to wait.

"So tell me how that happened," said Jeremy.

"I tripped over." A reluctance to discuss the details stole over Grace. Something to do with Jeremy's dislike of Harry? But why should she feel protective of Harry?

"How? Where?" he demanded.

"In the front doorway."

But Jeremy wasn't satisfied. "You mean you just fell over in the doorway?"

He wasn't a lawyer for nothing, she realized belatedly.

"Not exactly."

"Grace, for heavens sake tell me what happened," he said in exasperation

"I tripped over Woof. Harry's dog," she said.

"What was the dog doing in the doorway? Were you taking him for a walk or looking after him for that man?"

"No. I'd been baby sitting William, actually. Harry wasn't home and William didn't know where else to go after school, so he came over to my place." She stopped as she realized how bad that made Harry sound.

"Go on," said Jeremy in a calm voice. His witness coaxing voice. She'd heard him use it on a poor, stumbling, red faced woman in court who contradicted herself every time she opened her mouth.

"Harry came home and William and I went outside. Woof came down the path to greet me. He likes me," she added as if it were some sort of excuse. "And when I turned to go inside to get William's school bag I tripped over Woof."

"So the dog was on your property, unrestrained," stated Jeremy.

"Yes, I suppose so."

"No suppose about it Grace, it was, from what you've just said."

Grace nodded and bit her lip. Why was Jeremy cross examining her like this? The damage had been done.

"It was an accident," she protested weakly.

"A preventable accident. And you obviously can't work," he said.

"No. They've given me sick leave for six weeks."

"And after that?"

She shrugged.

"And how much physical therapy will you need?"

"I'm not sure. It depends how well it heals."

"Or if it heals. You have to face the prospect, Grace," he said gently, "that it might not heal at all to the point where you can play as well again. To a professional level."

"I know. I have thought about it Jeremy, I'm not an idiot."

"You may well lose your job. And do you have adequate medical insurance? For therapy over an extended period?"

Grace shook her head. "I have basic hospital cover insurance."

"Won't cover much at all. If anything. You're not in hospital and when you go in through the emergency room, Medicare picks up the tab."

"What are you getting at Jeremy?" asked Grace

"What I'm getting at Grace," he said firmly. "Is that you have a very good case to sue the irresponsible bastard."

Chapter Eight

"I couldn't do that!" Grace cried in horror.

"Don't let yourself be walked over," said Jeremy sternly.

Grace stared at him. Was that what she was doing? Was the reluctance to sue simply Old Grace being weak and unwilling to assert herself? Or was the reluctance to sue New Grace not wanting to be pushed into something that felt all wrong?

"Come and see me in my office and we'll work out the details. You'll need to tell me everything you can remember. I'll get my secretary to call you on Monday and make an appointment. Don't forget to bring in your x-rays and any paperwork from the hospital."

"I don't think I can afford to hire you, Jeremy,"

protested Grace but he waved her words away like an annoying insect. And getting his secretary to call sounded as though he thought she wouldn't, if left to her own devices. Jeremy was taking over again.

"We take a cut of the settlement. No need to worry about legal costs at this stage. What we need to decide is what sort of case you have and how much we can expect to get. And then double it!" Jeremy raised his glass and toasted her. "Cheers!"

"No!" cried Grace and Jeremy startled her by laughing gleefully and saying, "Just kidding, Grace. Don't worry. It's not a personal attack on your neighbor if that's what you're concerned about."

"Not personal?"

"No, no. If he's as smart as you say, he'll see you deserve to be compensated for your injury. It's a dog eat dog world Grace and you're altogether too naïve." Jeremy shoved a piece of garlic bread into his mouth and wiped his fingers on his napkin.

Grace sat through the rest of dinner in a daze. Food and drink passed her lips, Jeremy talked incessantly, he paid the bill, and the next she knew they were in the sporty blue machine again.

"Tired?" he asked. "You've been very quiet all evening."

"Yes." She added, "My arm's aching," and flicked a little smile in his direction so as to stop any probes into her mental state, which at this moment was still in shock. How could she sue Harry? The whole idea was repellent, repugnant in the extreme. Grace glanced at Jeremy's profile in the semi-darkness.

Light from streetlights and other cars illuminated his features at intermittent intervals and he had a smug look of satisfaction on his face that she recognized of old. Things were going his way, Jeremy was on top, in charge. Resentment stirred in her belly. How could she have ever thought she loved this man? He made his living out of other people's misfortune. He took pleasure and pride in getting some crook a reduced sentence or even a pardon. Even as she thought it, Grace's innate sense of fairplay told her that wasn't strictly true or fair. Lawyers were necessary to protect people's rights and to see they were given justice in what could be termed a very unfair society.

Look at her own case, for example. Tripped over a dog and as a result may lose her livelihood, no, more than that, music was her vocation, her life, and her greatest love. She may lose everything. Her life may never be the same again and all because Harry didn't keep his dog on a leash. He said sorry but that won't heal her wrist or pay her bills. Where's the justice in that? Maybe Jeremy was right. Harry owed her big time.

"Not personal?" she queried again in a completely different tone of voice this time and Jeremy must have known immediately she was referring to the conversation over dinner, two hours ago.

"Come and see me next week," said Jeremy and

smiled as he reached across and patted her on the knee. "By the way, love your new look. Short skirts suit you." And he gave a little tiger growl.

She lifted her sling marginally and grimaced to show him it still hurt to move.

He sighed. "All right, Princess."

Harry settled down to work on his book. Words were flowing easily. That happened sometimes and he was loathe to stop. That's why he hadn't gone to Italian on Monday. Part of the reason anyway. The other he kept hidden away at the back of his mind with all the other shameful things he'd put in there and tried not to think about.

Saturday morning. Alone because William had a sleepover and party today at a friend's house and it all became too difficult if he was to come back to Harry's this weekend. He'd be there now. Harry had left him in the midst of an excited group of little boys at some brave, or foolhardy, parent's house an hour earlier.

The phone rang and Harry got up reluctantly to answer it. He filled the electric kettle one handed as Janis said, "Hello, Harry."

"Hello. Is everything all right?"

"Yes, yes. Why do you always think I'm calling to complain?" Her voice had that snappish quality that set his teeth on edge. He dumped the filled jug on the counter and switched it on.

"Sorry," he said quietly.

He could hear her breathing in the space before she said, “I know. I’m sorry.” Harry bit his lip. “Harry, can we meet? I need to talk to you. It’s important. Are you at home today?”

“Yes.” Harry’s heart stalled. She was getting married. She was marrying and installing a new father in his place.

“Can I come over?”

“Can’t you tell me over the phone?” he asked harshly.

“I’d rather not. I’ll be over in thirty minutes. Okay?” She waited for his reply and he said, defeated, “Pick up some bread on the way. I’m just boiling the kettle.”

“See you soon.” And she hung up.

Harry began making a pot of coffee but stopped and wandered out into the yard. Woof bounded up with wagging tail but Harry ignored him and paced about, oblivious to the hot sun beating down on his bare head. He heard the screen door bang next door and Grace came out. He could see her upper body as she walked across to the birch tree. She had on a big floppy straw hat with a bright pink fake flower on it. Silly and pretty. It matched the pink of her cast. She’d worn it to Italian that day he’d been angry and not offered her a ride home in the heat. Being petty.

She disappeared below the fence line and he imagined her reclining on one of those rickety looking garden chairs they had or sprawling on the grass sunning herself. Tanning those shapely legs with the plum colored nail polish and the silver ankle bracelet he'd noticed her wearing sometimes.

Harry walked across to the fence and peered over. She had on shorts and she sat crosslegged on a blanket in the shade studying a book. She had a pen in her hand and an open notebook on her lap.

"Hello, Grace," Harry called softly.

Her head shot up and the pink flower bobbed and flapped. She had on dark glasses so he couldn't properly read her expression.

"Morning," she said in a strained sounding voice.

"How are you?" he asked.

"Okay. Considering."

Harry didn't know what to answer to that so he groped wildly and came up with, "I didn't get to class on Monday. Had a flow of inspiration for the book and didn't want to lose it. What did we do?"

"We learned how to tell each other we'd broken our arm and that we had to go to the hospital. How to say 'I'm in pain' and 'I need to see a doctor.' "

Harry winced. "Grace . . ."

"Chapter four. We have to translate the exercises at the end of Chapter four," she said ignoring his interruption.

"Oh, thanks."

"It's about the present tense of verbs ending in a-r-e."

"Difficult?" he asked.

"Complicated." Grace sighed. "I wonder if Italians remember all those grammar rules?"

"Doubt it. They all speak dialects anyway. We're probably learning high class sounding Italian."

Grace smiled at his attempt at a truce and Harry grinned back in relief.

"Roberto won't ever sound high class," he added and Grace actually laughed.

"Neither will you," she said, but he knew she was kidding.

"My accent's better than his."

"True. Just."

Harry heard a car door slam and the smile left his face abruptly.

"Glad you're feeling better," he said. "I have to go. A visitor." He pulled a face to hide the dismay and the dread in his stomach. "Janis."

They both heard the knock at the front door. Harry waved to Grace and ran across the grass and in the back door. He ran a cold, clammy hand through his hair as he hurried through the house. Janis stood on the step, cool, calm and holding a bag of groceries.

"Come in," he said and kissed her proffered cheek quickly. "You didn't need to empty the deli."

"It's nothing," she said. Her voice sounded tight. She must be nervous about telling him he'd been replaced. Well, he wasn't going to make it easy for her.

She followed him to the kitchen where she carefully put the bag on the table and began unpacking it. Harry got out plates and knives and finished making the pot of coffee he'd begun when she rang. He watched her blond head bent over the plate of salami and ham she was preparing.

"I got the spicy Hungarian, I know you like that," she said without looking at him.

"Janis," he said sharply. "What do you have to tell me?"

She sat down and looked at him then. This wasn't like her. She was usually very direct, had no problem stating her intentions.

"Spit it out," he said.

"I'm leaving Sydney. I've been offered a job in Melbourne and then possibly I'll have to move to the U.S. in the middle of next year. I'll be travelling. A lot." She stared at him as first relief, then dismay, and then a wild optimism flooded through his body.

"William?" The word barely came out, a whisper of sound.

"I think it would be best if he came to live with you. School, and his friends and everything. Better for him. If you agree." Janis stared up at him. He knew what was going through her head. She was expecting him to berate her for putting her career ahead of her son the way he'd done through the last bitter years of their marriage. But she couldn't have been more wrong.

"Agree?" he shouted. "Agree? Of course I agree." He lunged forward and scooped her up to hug her tightly. She clung to him and laughed.

"I thought you might."

Harry let Janis go. "Does he know?"

"He knows I was applying for a better position in the firm but no, he doesn't know about the move."

"I don't know whether to laugh or cry," said Harry. "I thought you were going to come and tell me you were getting married and that there'd be some other guy moving in."

Janis laughed. "Harry, Harry. This is me, Miss Super Career Woman. Remember? Never should have gotten married in the first place?"

Harry did. Another one of those remarks he wished would remain in the past. He hung his head.

"I'm sorry. I was . . . I've no excuse. I'm sorry."

Janis said quietly, "You may well have been right, you know? Don't get me wrong. I loved you and I adore William, I'd never regret having him but for me, marriage doesn't seem right." She shrugged. "You always wanted the type of home I couldn't possibly provide."

"We made a mistake."

"Yes," she said.

"Hey!" Harry cried suddenly. "Congratulations. You've landed a top job by the sound of it. Tell me about it."

And so Janis did and when she left a couple of hours later, Harry picked her a bunch of roses and said, "That was the happiest we've been together for years. Now I remember why I wanted to marry you."

Janis took the roses and put her arms around Harry to hold him close. He felt her body shaking and when he released her and looked into her eyes he saw the glint of tears. She smiled sheepishly. "I'll miss you Harry."

"You'll miss William more," he said. "You just wait."

"Yes, I probably will but I know he'll be in the best possible hands."

"Call me when you know dates and details," Harry said. "William can move in any time."

He waved as Janis drove away and when he started to walk back down the path he suddenly changed his mind and went to Grace's instead. He didn't examine why. He knocked and a few minutes later heard her step in the hallway.

"William's coming to live with me," he cried as soon as the door opened. "Janis is moving to Melbourne in a few weeks and next year she's going to America. With work."

Grace's expression changed from astonishment to real, genuine delight.

"That's wonderful," she said. The smile faded. "Why are you telling me?"

Harry stared at her wordlessly then flung his arms out helplessly. "I don't know. I've no idea. I thought you might be interested but there's no reason why you would be. Sorry. I'll go."

He turned and almost ran down the path and along to his own front gate. Grace watched him go. She smiled to herself and shook her head before closing the door with a gentle click. Then she leaned against it.

Lucky Harry. Everything falling neatly into place for him. But that was an unworthy thought. Grace pulled herself up sharply. She didn't resent Harry's regaining of his son. She was pleased for him. Delighted for him, delighted to see him so happy. It was wonderful news and William must be pleased about it too. Although he'd be sure to miss his mom and vice-versa.

That would mean she'd get to see more of William as well. He'd be over here often enough that was for sure and she could babysit for Harry when he had his classes or went out. On dates. Did Harry go out on dates?

Not that she knew. She didn't spy of course but he didn't go out at night and she'd been his last date. Grace remembered with an intense stab of desire and longing the way Harry had kissed her. No-one had kissed her like that and made her feel like that. No-one. Not even Jeremy at the height of their affair. And wasn't it true to form that the one man who could turn her inside out spent his spare time insulting and belittling her and wanted less than nothing to do with her? And her own feelings were ambivalent towards him at best, swinging wildly from intense desire and a sort of love to intense dislike. But she couldn't bear the thought of him kissing someone else the way he'd kissed her.

Grace pushed herself away from the door and wandered to the kitchen. Eric was making a cup of tea. The orchestra had a concert tonight and he'd spent the afternoon asleep. They'd performed last night too while she'd been out with Jeremy.

"Who was that?" he asked.

"Harry. He came to tell me William is moving in with him permanently. His mother's moving out of town." Grace flopped down on a chair and rested her head on her good hand.

"Cool," said Eric. "Great kid. Why didn't you ask him in?"

"He seemed to be in a hurry," said Grace. "Just told me and then took off."

"How was the date with the jerk?" asked Eric. He dragged the cookie jar towards him and examined the contents. "Make oatmeal ones next time, Grace."

"Okay," she said answering both requests at the same time. "Jeremy thinks I should sue Harry for damages."

"Wow. Heavy."

"I know but all the physical therapy and stuff will cost a fortune and what if I can't play again professionally?"

Eric nodded. "How much will you get does he think?"

"I have to go and see him on Monday and give him all the details and then he'll figure it out. Then double it he said but he was joking, I hope."

Eric dunked his cookie and it fell apart in his tea. He picked up a teaspoon and began fishing out soggy lumps and slurping them into his mouth. Grace watched. Irritation grew and spread like a cancerous lump. Irritation not just with Eric and his questionable table manners but with her whole frustrating, worrying situation and the whole frustrating thing with Harry who she didn't know whether to love or hate, blame or forgive.

"You really are disgusting, you know that?" she said.

Eric stared at her, surprise and the beginnings of annoyance spreading across his features.

"You never used to be this picky, Grace. Certainly not so vindictive as to consider suing someone. And not just anyone—Harry, our friend and neighbor," said Eric. "You've changed. You know that?" He got up. Grace had never seen him so angry. They'd never argued, that she could remember, even as children. Unfamiliar little red spots burned in his cheeks.

"My livelihood was never threatened before and I changed deliberately remember? So that people wouldn't use me as a doormat. Like now."

"Harry's not using you as a doormat, he's a naturally friendly person—like you used to be," cried Eric. "What's he supposed to do? And he likes you, the poor fool."

"He does not! That's ridiculous." Stupid Eric. What did he know?

"Why else would he come rushing over here to tell you about William? He can't take his eyes off you when he is here, he's always bringing you roses and you treated him like dirt right from the word go."

Grace stared speechless as Eric grew more and more verbose and seemed to swell before her astounded eyes.

"And another thing! If you can change one way, you can change back. Marcel's right. You upset the natural balance the way you've been carrying on."

"Right. The natural balance being that a woman is a threat if she becomes more assertive so keep her back in the kitchen where she belongs," Grace yelled finding her voice at last.

"That's garbage Grace and you know it. You're a talented, professional, respected woman. There's a difference between being that and losing all semblance of yourself as a person, burying your natural personality under a load of contrived mannerisms and aggression or whatever. If you want to be the best violinist in the world, go for it. If you like cooking and pottering around the house, go for it. If you want to have kids and stop work to raise them, go for it but don't try to be something you're not. Be yourself while you're doing whatever it is. The leopard can't change its spots, Grace."

"But I was a disaster as myself," wailed Grace.

"You were not! Just because that lawyer thought you were too easy going means nothing. Says more about him than you. Uptight moron."

"Well, how come I'm still single?"

"It's not a measure of you as a person whether you're single or not!"

"I know, I know. I'm a mess, Eric," said Grace dismally, collapsing.

"Yup," he said dropping back down on to his chair. "Have another cup of tea."

Eric slurped his tea and soggy cookie and Grace smiled forlornly and dunked her own cookie.

"Did you mean that?" she asked after a few minutes silence. Eric cocked an eyebrow interrogatively. "About Harry? You know." Grace felt the flush rising steadily up her throat and into her cheeks. Eric grinned.

"Go and see for yourself. I bet I'm right."

"I can't do that! And since when have you known anything about the subject?"

"I'm not the insensitive neanderthal you think I am. Invite him over tonight to keep you company."

"Eric!"

"I've got to go and iron my shirt." He added as an afterthought, "You may have blown it, of course."

Eric got up and sauntered out. She yelled after him, "What makes you think I'm interested in *him*?" but received no reply.

Grace sat with her cheeks burning and her brain trying to sort out the implications of what Eric had just dumped in her lap. She'd been so busy figuring out how to manage New Grace with her attitude and her ambition she hadn't considered that Harry might really be attracted to her.

How did she feel about Harry in the light of that?

Grace wasn't sure. Wasn't sure at all. Confused

would be the aptest description. Attracted was in there somewhere. Very attracted right from the start. Harry had little lines around his mouth that made her insides go weak and his eyes were fringed with dark lashes. His body fitted hers perfectly as proven when they danced and when he hugged her. Harry was kind and gentle and loving and caring. He had proven that with how he treated William and how he cared for her when she was injured.

Grace sat still and remembered the way he'd held her hand at the hospital and how he washed her feet and held her when she cried. And the way he held her when they danced together at the dinner and how he looked at her sometimes. Deep, penetrating, searching looks that made her uncomfortable but in a pleasantly tingling sort of way.

And Harry, apart from the devastating kiss he had so casually bestowed and then so casually undermined with that wink, had never shown the slightest interest in being with her or going out together. He'd been polite and neighborly. But why had he kissed her? He said he wanted to see what it was like but men don't kiss women unless they're interested in them. Men like Harry, anyway. She couldn't imagine him doing or saying that to Camilla the predator. Could he have been jealous of Jeremy?

He seemed to respond to her most when she was in some sort of predicament. So was Harry only interested in a helpless, dopey woman who couldn't look after herself? Even Old Grace had never been that sort of girl. Fluttering eyelashes and 'please help poor little me' types made her want to throw up. Surely he couldn't be one of those men, not Harry. She'd always thought men who fell for that line were the biggest dopes on earth. And Harry was no dope.

Now with all that to chew over what was she going to do about it, if anything, and what was Harry going to do about it? From his side the answer appeared to be nothing. Eric may well have got it right—she'd scared Harry off. New Grace had.

That night Grace sat alone watching television. Boring. She turned it off and picked up the book she'd started, flipped the pages and tried to remember what it was about. None of the characters were familiar. She tossed it aside and turned on the radio. Brahms flowed into the room. Brahms' *Requiem Mass.* Beautiful, but too depressing right now. She twiddled the dial and came up with some pop and some heavy rock and some country music and someone talking earnestly about cloning and she clicked it off.

After the heat of the day had come a hot still, airless night with the sort of charge in the atmosphere that precedes a storm. Grace opened the front door and wandered down the path taking deep breaths of the rose perfumed air. The thick, heavy smell seemed to sit like a cloud over their front gardens. Lights were on in Harry's house. He'd be in there with William being thrashed at Monopoly. Lucky, lucky Harry to have such a wonderful son, to have a family.

His front door opened suddenly casting a shaft of yellow light into the garden and she heard him say something. The door closed and Harry appeared with Woof on his leash. They turned out the gate in her direction. Grace froze. He might not notice her standing here in the darkness. But Woof did. He gave a little yip of welcome and his tail started waving like a banner.

Her face felt as hot as a furnace. Thank goodness for the darkness. Perspiration ran in beads down her back under her skimpy singlet top and into the waistband of her shorts. Her cast in the sling was stifling.

"Grace?" Harry's voice came softly. He stopped by the lopsided gate and Woof sniffed the air, his tail still wagging.

"Hello," she said. "It's so hot. I came out for some air."

"Me too. There may be a storm." His voice was calm and noncommittal. Hardly the tone of a man fighting to suppress an overwhelming passion for the woman before him.

"Where's William?" she asked.

"At a sleepover party. He only stayed last night with me."

Grace moved forward and patted Woof on the head. He licked her hand and she laughed softly and tousled his ears.

"So you forgive him?" asked Harry.

"It wasn't his fault," said Grace quickly and then bit her lip as the obvious follow up seemed to be that the fault was Harry's. She felt rather than saw his body stiffen and he gave a gentle tug on the lead. Woof stepped back and looked up at him.

"Come on," he said and turned. "Good night, Grace."

"Harry!" Grace called impulsively. "Harry, can I come with you? Please?"

Harry hesitated and Grace said, "It's so hot . . . I'd like to go for a walk but not by myself . . . at night."

"All right."

"Wait a minute while I lock up?"

"Sure."

Grace raced inside, grabbed her keys, checked the back door and was back panting beside Harry and Woof in less than two minutes. They began strolling and Grace struggled to slow her breathing and get her thoughts in order. She wasn't quite sure what she wanted to say to him now. And he was different suddenly. The Harry she knew before harbored a deep dislike of her whole outlook on life, or rather what he thought was her skewed outlook on life. Now with her final sloughing off of Jeremy, her re-embracing of Old Grace and Eric's idea germinating and flourishing in her mind, the reality of Harry as a boyfriend became very attractive and very possible.

Grace realized with a shock of awareness he'd been sitting there quietly in the background for quite some time, in fact, establishing himself in her head and she wanted very much to encourage that Harry who rather liked her. She wanted to fan that ember into desperately in love Harry. She wanted more kisses like the one in the elevator. Without an audience next time. She wanted to know all about Harry. But the figure pacing silently beside her made her shy and tongue-tied. Maybe he despised her and she'd blown her chance before she even realized there was one.

Harry walked slowly in the darkness unbearably conscious of Grace close beside him. Their shoulders brushed occasionally and sometimes his bare arm rubbed against her bare arm and he was made breathless by the electricity of the contact. Her skin was hot against his at those odd moments and he could smell her perfume, light and fresh in the oppressive atmosphere.

She seemed oblivious, lost in her own thoughts.

He hoped she wasn't about to say something that would spoil their walk. He'd had enough tension and emotional upheavals today and over the last few weeks for that matter. He'd planned a quiet, long walk to think about William and Janis and to ponder the progress of his book. He didn't want to think about Grace. That topic was too complicated, too mixed up with desire and longing and a love that would be not only stupid, messy and doomed but was, as far as he could gather, unrequited, which in itself was probably just as well.

"Harry, I've never had much success with relationships," Grace began and Harry was so startled he said nothing for about six paces. Grace didn't follow up her remark with an explanation so he said, "I suppose I haven't either."

"At least you found someone who wanted to marry you. I've never even got close and I'm nearly 31," she said and sounded so miserable Harry nearly groaned aloud as his own cruel words played back in his head. Luckily she continued on without referring to that day. "And you've got William. I'd love to have a child."

"Would you?" Harry asked before he could erase the complete surprise from his voice.

"Yes," she replied sharply doing one of those personality about faces that confirmed his original opinion of her. "Is that so amazing?"

"But I thought you were determined to advance in the orchestra. That sort of ambition doesn't leave much room for children." He knew that from bitter experience.

"No," she said and again didn't continue.

"So didn't it work out with the lawyer?" he asked lightly. "Despite my best efforts."

"Yes and no," replied Grace and Harry frowned in the darkness. He wished he hadn't probed, wished he'd had the resistance not to care what had happened between Grace and that cheese ball who'd whirled her off in the sports car last night. Wished he hadn't lain in bed wondering . . .

"It brought on a date, didn't it?" he asked, twisting the knife a little more.

A sheet of lightning followed almost immediately by a clap of thunder drowned out any reply from Grace and Harry said, “We’d better get home quickly. It’s going to pour any minute.”

Another roar of thunder underlined his words and they began to run, with Woof prancing and dancing in front of them and the sky rent by jagged prongs of light. The tumult in the sky seemed to Harry to match the tumult in his heart and his mind as they hurried along the path because Grace had placed her hand in his and gripped tightly, but the contradiction and ambiguity of her words resounded in his head, like alarm bells.

Chapter Nine

They reached Grace's front gate as the first big, cool drops began to fall. Grace let Harry's hand go and ran down the path to unlock the front door. She flung it open and turned to usher Harry in but was dismayed to see him with Woof, running along the footpath in a dash for home.

"Come in," she called taking a few steps out into the rain which had fast become more than just a few drops.

"No thanks," shouted Harry."May as well get home. Woof stinks when he's wet."

He waved and she watched as he unlocked his own door and disappeared inside. She darted back into shelter and went to the bathroom for a towel to wipe the dampness from her hair. She'd have to change her top too. At least it was cool now. She wished Harry had come in. Why hadn't he? Eric was wrong.

Ten minutes later someone thumped on the door.

Grace paused with her hand on the lock and the towel draped over her arm. She called loudly, "Who is it?"

"Harry."

She flung the door wide and Harry stood there on the step with water dripping from a large black umbrella.

"Hello." The word barely came out. Her throat had gone dry.

"Hello." He furled the umbrella and propped it against the outside wall. "Can I come in?"

"Yes, of course." Grace stepped back quickly. Harry walked in. He stood close to her as she closed the door.

Grace couldn't move. Her heart thumped in her chest and she gazed at him like a hypnotized rabbit. What was he doing here? Why had he come back? She'd wanted him to. Would he kiss her again? She couldn't just launch herself at him Camilla style.

"Grace?"

She blinked. Her brain restarted. "Oh. Sorry. I was about to change my top."

"Can you manage?" he asked softly and Grace's startled gaze flew to his eyes, gray and gentle as he looked down at her. She nodded and fled to her bedroom.

Harry leaned against the wall in the hallway and took a deep, shaky breath. What on earth was he doing here? She was amazed that he'd come back, he could see it in her expression when she opened the door. He wanted to kiss her. He wanted to hold her and feel the warmth of her body in his arms. He wanted to taste her lips again and he wanted to drive the image of that blasted lawyer of hers right out of her head.

That's why he was here. But he couldn't just grab her, she'd scream blue murder.

Grace came out of her bedroom wearing a blouse, an ethnic looking embroidered cotton thing. Her hair was all loose and soft around her face, fluffy from where she'd been rubbing it dry with the towel. Harry straightened up. She was gorgeous. Simply no other way to put it.

"Did you leave Woof at home?" she said. Her cheeks immediately flushed. "That was a dopey thing to say. Of course you have."

"Yes," Harry said and grinned at her pink confusion. He folded his arms to stop himself reaching for her.

"What . . . did you want?" asked Grace.

Harry's mind went blank. Excuse, he needed an excuse. He hadn't felt like this since he was fifteen and manufacturing reasons to stroll by Emma Hicks's house after school.

"Italian," he blurted. "Can you help me with last week's lesson? Please?" He smiled in relief. Good one!

Grace smiled. Relief on her face too? "I don't know whether I'll be much use. But we can try," she said. "Coffee? Tea?"

"Yes," said Harry. Grace laughed and went to the kitchen with Harry trailing behind like a lovesick schoolboy.

"Where's your book?" she asked.

"Be back in a minute," said Harry. By the time he returned, panting and clutching his textbook and notebook, Grace had made tea and placed a plate of homemade cookies on the kitchen table. Her own Italian book was open and a school notebook lay beside it, the pages filled with her neat writing.

"Page eighteen," said Grace and sat down next to him. Close, so that his bare arm touched hers and he could smell the heady, sweet scent of her.

Harry flipped his own book open. Present tense of verbs ending in '–are'. Grace began to explain and Harry didn't take in one word. He couldn't take his eyes off her face bent studiously over the open text and her brow wrinkled slightly in concentration as she struggled to comprehend the intricacies of conjugating verbs.

"We have to memorize the endings," she said and looked up suddenly. Harry's eyes met hers and such a spark flew between them his heart stopped and started and then lurched on its way twice as fast as before. He picked up the mug of tea she'd poured and drank thirstily.

Grace returned to her explanations, her hair falling in a dark curtain obscuring her cheek. He longed to reach out and brush it aside and then run his fingertips over the soft line of her jaw and down her throat where he could see a pulse beating softly.

"Lots of verbs end in '–are,' " Grace said. "*Parlare*—to speak, *fumare*—to smoke, *ricordare*—to remember . . ." She looked up at him again and her voice faltered . . . stopped. A flush rose slowly up her neck. Was she remembering what he was remembering? Harry smiled at the way her lips curved and the way she was that gentle, vulnerable woman again. The one he'd told was lovely standing so forlornly in the front garden that first day. He wanted to kiss her so much it hurt.

He looked at the next word on the list.

"*Baciare*—to kiss," he whispered and leaned forward. His lips met hers and he closed his eyes and drank in the taste of her. He held her face gently between both palms feeling the heat of her skin and then with exhilaration the increasing heat of her kiss. She shifted slightly and her arm wrapped around his neck to draw him closer.

A crack of thunder startled her. Grace's eyes snapped open as she felt Harry jerk with surprise. He drew away. Lightning flashed and lit up the back yard. Grace stared at his face so close and so wonderful with the evidence of his passion glowing in his eyes. The lights flickered off and on. Harry sat back.

"Maybe the gods are telling us we shouldn't be doing this," he said softly.

"Why?" cried Grace.

Harry studied her face and said nothing and Grace

asked again, "Why, Harry? Because you think I'm attractive but that's as far as you want to go or because . . . you don't really like me?" Her voice failed her on the last words and she quickly brushed her hand across her eyes.

"No! I don't think that, Grace. William likes you and that's enough for me. No, that came out wrong. I like you, Grace, and I think you're the sexiest, most beautiful woman I've . . ." He shook his head. "But I don't want to get tangled up with anyone else. It's too soon after Janis and I'm just getting myself and William sorted out."

Grace nodded. "I understand," she said coldly. "Perfectly."

Harry grabbed her hand, gazed into her eyes. "Do you? Do you really Grace?"

"Oh yes," said Grace. "We'll be friends, shall we?"

Harry sighed. He stood up. "Thanks for the help."

"No problem. I'll see you at class, shall I?"

"*Si, certo*."

He gathered up his books

Grace followed him to the front door. There went another man who couldn't get out of her house fast enough. She'd failed again and after only one kiss. What did she have to do? New Grace was just as much, if not more, of a disaster than Old Grace. And this time it hurt even more because this time she'd fallen in love—harder and more convincingly than ever before. As soon as he kissed her she knew, the tentative surmising of earlier became fact. And the object of her affection thought she was unstable and not safe to have around his son. Hadn't put it into words quite so bluntly but that's what he meant. Time for a bit of Camilla style effrontery?

Harry paused at the open door. It was pouring outside. Streaks of lightning crackled through the darkness accompanied by growling and grumbling from the heavens.

"The gods are still angry," said Grace. "Maybe they don't want you to leave." She moved right up close to Harry and put her good arm around his neck. She stretched up on tiptoes and kissed him on the lips. She felt his body stiffen and then slowly he began to kiss her back. Grace closed her eyes and focused on the sensations shooting through her own body, making her tremble, weak with love and desire.

His fingers spread across the back of her neck and into her hair and she gave a small whimper of delight as the other hand reached around her back and held her tightly. Harry stopped.

"Sorry. I forgot . . . your arm . . ." he said thickly. Grace swam to the surface in a bewildered haze.

"It doesn't hurt," she whispered. "Harry?"

"Grace, I really don't think this is a good idea," he murmured. "I mean, it is and it isn't. I could stand here kissing you and it would lead to, who knows . . . and neither of us want that, do we? And you . . ."

"Me what?" asked Grace.

"You're irresistible," he said and kissed her lightly.

"What if I love you?" said Grace softly and held her breath.

Harry stared deep into her eyes. "But you don't," he said just as softly. "I'd be a great disappointment to you, Grace. I'm not ambitious, I don't earn vast amounts of money, I live a quiet life with my dog, my writing and now my son."

"And there's no room for a woman like . . . me," said Grace.

Harry shook his head. "It's not that . . . it's . . . it wouldn't work . . . we're too different. I tried that before, with Janis."

Grace cried desperately, "But I'm not like that Harry, like Janis. I'm not a career driven woman. You just caught me trying to be different. I decided I was too easy going and dull. And I messed up trying to be assertive. That's when you came along and got the worst of it. But I'm not like that really. Ask Eric."

Harry smiled and placed his palm against her cheek.

"Two weeks ago you were desperately in love with that lawyer. You're a beautiful nut," he said and picked up his umbrella. "Too confusing for me. *Ciao*."

"*Ciao*," called Grace miserably as she watched him splash down the path and across to his house. He waved and disappeared inside.

* * *

It poured solidly all Sunday. Eric came into the kitchen mid-morning, sleepy and dishevelled in search of coffee. He peered into Grace's mixing bowl.

"Is that a chocolate cake?"

"Yes," she said abruptly. "Get your fingers out of it." She slapped the back of his hand sharply and he retreated with a shocked expression and his chocolatey fingers in his mouth.

"What's up with you?"

"It's the last time I take your advice," said Grace.

"Why? What advice?" he demanded.

"You said Harry liked me and now he thinks I'm an idiot."

"What did you do?" asked Eric in a resigned voice. He dumped cereal into a bowl.

"Harry kissed me."

"So?"

"That's all. He doesn't want to become entangled with a nut like me."

"Is that what he said?" asked Eric looking up in surprise.

"In a nutshell, yes." Grace laughed and then stopped abruptly and went back to spooning cake mixture into an oven pan which was awkward with one functioning hand. A few tears plopped into the mixture and she sniffed and picked up the hand towel to wipe her eyes.

Eric got up and put his arms around her. "You are a nut for trying to change," he said. "There was nothing wrong with you before. It's all that awful Jeremy's fault!" He kissed her cheek then went back to his cereal.

"What am I going to do?" Grace wailed.

"I take it this means you care about Harry?" asked Eric

"Yes! Why would I be so upset otherwise?"

"Just getting things clear," said Eric mildly.

"Well?"

"What?"

"What am I going to do?"

Eric pulled a face. "Beats me," he said. "Anyway you said it was the last time you'd take my advice."

Grace put the cake pan into the oven and set the timer. "That's right," she said. "You're no help to man nor beast."

"Yup, that's me. But I play a mean trombone." He spooned a few mouthfuls in and chewed thoughtfully. "The orchestra is going on that tour," he said.

"Asia?" Grace's heart fell. The trip had been in the wind but no-one knew for certain. China, Hong Kong, Japan and the Philippines. "When?"

"Next June and July."

"I should be better by then," she said hopefully, staring at her cast. "This thing comes off in a couple more weeks and with physical therapy . . . don't you think?'

"Don't know. You'd think so, though. It's seven or eight months away."

"I really want to go," Grace said.

"So do I."

But did she really want to go and leave Harry for two months? Even if he didn't love her like she loved him he would be next door and she'd see him almost every day. But he was going to Italy next year. What about William? And Woof.

They weren't her problem, Harry had made that very clear.

Grace walked to Italian the next morning carrying a red umbrella with a wooden duck's head handle. It wasn't actually raining but big gray clouds swirled about threateningly and the air was still hot. The gods obviously hadn't finished their business.

"*Buon giorno,* Grace," called Roberto as soon as she appeared. His accent hadn't improved. Even Harry sounded better. Especially when he said *baciare*.

"*Ciao*, Roberto," murmured Grace and sat down across the table and at the far end. Myra came in next followed by the rest of the group and Franco. Myra sat beside Grace and studied her quietly. Grace shifted uncomfortably under the intense scrutiny. Would Harry turn up today? She felt like giving Myra her palm to read. Perhaps she was reading her aura. It would be blue and possibly black. The colors of misery, anyhow.

"All will be well, Grace," she said suddenly in her otherworldly voice. "Your destiny cannot be altered." Fine if Harry featured in it. Otherwise . . .

"Thanks, Myra."

Harry came in at that moment and sat opposite Myra. She greeted him with a quiet smile and opened her text book. The lesson got underway. Franco began asking them to conjugate '–are' verbs, one by one around the table. He reached Harry.

"You missed this lesson," he said.

"It's all right, Grace helped me," Harry said and flicked a smile at Grace. Her lips trembled in response and she had to look away.

"*Amare*—to love," announced Franco and looked expectantly at Harry. "I love," he prompted.

"*Amo,*" said Harry. "*Ame, ama. Amiamo, amate, amiono.*"

"*Ami,*" corrected Franco. "You singular love is '*ami*' "

"*Ami,*" repeated Harry and looked straight at Grace with a big grin. "You love."

Grace's face was in danger of spontaneous combustion. Now he was teasing her, in public.

"Excuse me," she said and stood up quickly to escape to the ladies.

When she returned with cooler cheeks and a determined, New Grace stride they had moved on to discuss vocabulary dealing with pets and Roberto was telling them in fractured Italian mixed with bits of English about his cat named Mimi which only ate chicken and meat from a certain butcher in the next suburb.

Myra gave her a sphinxlike smile as she took her place. Grace knew Harry was watching her trying not to look at him. And laughing. It must be very amusing to have a woman say she loves you. Grace and Camilla.

He'd be able to use them both in one of his books, the basis for a dysfunctional alien character.

Harry approached her during their break but Grace made a point of talking to Liz about her baby and he went off to sit with Franco and Myra. Going home was another matter. Harry had walked to class as well and Grace had no option but to walk with him, stiff and hideously self conscious. Even being berated by Jeremy in the front garden didn't match the humiliation she was experiencing now. What was he going to say about the other night?

Harry, by contrast appeared very chirpy. The reason was soon made apparent.

"William's moving in next week," he said soon after they'd started walking.

"That's good."

"I can't wait." Harry's voice held a wealth of love and satisfaction and Grace's heart turned over with longing to be the object of such tenderness—his tenderness. She managed a smile.

"I can imagine. But he'll miss his mom, won't he?"

"Yes, he will but we'll keep in touch with e-mail and phone calls, letters."

"People don't write letters much any more," commented Grace. "I like getting letters. Real ones. And I love postcards with exotic pictures."

"So do I," said Harry. "And I write them too."

They walked in silence. She began to relax. Harry

was obviously not going to humiliate her further by alluding to Saturday night again. She forgot sometimes just how kind he could be. Grace shifted her purse on her shoulder. The Italian books made it heavy but she couldn't switch arms.

"I'm sorry," said Harry. "Let me take your bag." He slipped the strap from her shoulder and slung it over his arm before she could protest.

"Thanks. You don't have to . . . but thanks."

"No *problemo*," he said in Roberto's accent. Grace smiled.

"The orchestra's touring Asia next year," she said.

"That'll be interesting. Ever been?"

"No, I haven't been out of Australia. Unless you count Tasmania."

Harry laughed. "Hey, I'm from Hobart!"

"Are you?" Grace laughed as well. "That explains it then," she said and laughed again.

"You should be learning Japanese or Chinese instead of Italian," said Harry.

"I'll learn Chinese next," said Grace. "And then Japanese. That's of course, if I get to go at all."

"You will," said Harry. "When does the cast come off?"

"In three weeks. Then I'll have to go to physical therapy and do exercises to strengthen the tendons and things."

Harry said nothing. He didn't know what *to* say apart

from apologizing again. And Grace seemed different now after some initial tension in class when he did his conjugation of *amare* and teased her. Her clothes were different too he realized as he glanced at her walking beside him. She had on a long, printed Fijian skirt and a little, white, knitted top which showed her midriff. Her hair was in a ponytail and she looked about eighteen. But she certainly wasn't eighteen.

They reached his gate and Harry handed her her bag.

"Thanks Harry." She smiled into his eyes. "Like a cup of tea?"

"No, I'd better do some work, thanks. Been a bit slack lately what with . . ." He gestured vaguely and wished he was younger and less responsible and unaccountable for his actions in which case he'd idle away the rest of the day drinking tea with this lovely girl.

"All right. See you next week." And Grace went along to her own gate and disappeared into her house without a backward glance. Harry stared after her for a minute or two, the image of the swinging ponytail in his mind reinforcing her youthfulness. So much for a woman in love. Carefree, careless. Fickleness thy name is Grace. Friends it was.

Jeremy's secretary called later that afternoon. Grace told her politely that she wouldn't make an appointment after all. Jeremy came to see her himself on Saturday, sternfaced and businesslike.

"Why didn't you make an appointment?" he asked

when she'd sat him down with a drink in the living room. Eric had disappeared out the back door as soon as he heard Jeremy's voice. Grace felt like doing the same.

"I want to wait," she said in an attempt to put him off. "My arm might be perfectly all right in a couple of months."

"And if it isn't?"

"I'll think about it then."

Jeremy looked at her shrewdly. "You don't want to do anything about it, do you?"

Grace firmed her mouth into a straight line. "No. I don't."

"And it's because of that writer, isn't it?"

"Not just because of Harry. I don't think it's the right thing to do, suing someone when it was partly my fault. And I'd have to go to court. It'd be awful."

Jeremy shook his head in disgust. "You're too weak, Grace."

"I'm not weak, Jeremy," she cried. "I just have some moral scruples."

"That guy owes you. Where are his moral scruples? Doesn't he feel any responsibility for this at all? At least I'm trying to help you and you make me out to be the unscrupulous bloodsucking lawyer." Jeremy's voice raised to the familiar level of frustration that had typified their last encounters. He put his glass down and stood up.

"He can't afford it," said Grace. "He has a son to look after and a house to pay off."

"Well, he should be more careful, shouldn't he?" snapped Jeremy. He strode to the front door and yanked it open. "Call me when you get that cast off and you can't play properly. See who's the more responsible then. See which man you prefer then!"

"Jeremy," cried Grace. "This isn't a competition to see who's the best man. That's ridiculous. And you left me, remember!?"

"Ridiculous? I thought you were comparing us at that dinner. Goodbye," he said viciously and slammed the door as he left. This time Grace didn't run after him. She stood in the hallway breathing hard. Furious with Jeremy. Furious with herself.

Harry and William were in the front garden pulling weeds out of the rose bed when Grace's door slammed. Harry had recognized the blue car immediately and swallowed the toxic lump of bitterness and jealousy that threatened to choke him. He yanked weeds out imagining they were the entrails of the slick, good-looking so-and-so visiting Grace.

William chattered nonstop and took his mind marginally away from the subject until the crashing door made them both look up in surprise.

"Gosh," said William and giggled.

"Ssh," hissed Harry and frowned. What had that low-life said to Grace this time? Should he go in and see if she was all right? No. He couldn't, none of his business. Anyway Eric was home.

Jeremy paused as he passed Harry's gate. He looked

in and Harry saw the anger on his face and the quick glance he gave William.

"Can I have a word with your dad, please?"

William turned in astonishment to Harry. Harry nodded briefly and stood up. "Take the bucket around the back." He waited while William went off around the side of the house carrying the red plastic bucket full of weeds.

"What is it?" he asked warily.

"You're responsible for Grace's broken arm," said Jeremy coming straight to the point.

Harry didn't reply. He waited.

"You'd better hope it heals one hundred percent because if she is in anyway impaired she'll be hanging you out to dry."

"What do you mean by that?" asked Harry as a chill radiated slowly and inexorably through his entire body.

"What do I mean?" crowed Jeremy. "I mean, if Grace can't play her violin as well as she could before your dog tripped her up, then you'll be paying. She's going to sue you for every penny of her costs and then some. Better start praying or buying lotto tickets because the number I'm thinking will be six figures, at least."

Chapter Ten

Harry watched the blue car roar down the street. He couldn't move. The hand holding the weeding fork hung by his side and he shivered despite the heat of the afternoon. William came back with the empty bucket.

"Who was that?" he asked. "Was that Grace's friend?"

"Yes, that's Grace's boyfriend," said Harry in a low voice which even to his ears sounded full of bile. He cleared his throat.

"I don't like him," stated William. "I think you should be Grace's boyfriend."

Harry stared at William. "Do you?" he asked. "Why?"

"Because Grace is pretty and she's nice and she can cook really well. And we need someone like that now that Mom's not going to be here. And I'm too young to be her boyfriend"

Harry put his hand on William's shoulder and squeezed. "We'll be fine, you and I, William."

"And Woof."

"Yes, and Woof."

Harry began to pull out more weeds but Jeremy's words played ceaselessly in his head. Grace wanted to sue him? She'd never even hinted as much. Ever. That lawyer had put that idea in her head sure as eggs. She couldn't want to sue him. It was impossible!

But if her arm didn't heal . . . and she was unpredictable at the best of times.

Harry stopped working and sat back on the grass. He'd never be able to come up with a six figure amount. Not even high five figure amount. How much were they talking? He'd have to sell the house! And then what would happen to William? He'd be unable to provide a proper home and William would have to go back to Janis. And live in Melbourne or possibly overseas. No one wanted that. Not Janis, not William and definitely not Harry. He'd have to go to see Grace and find out for himself.

He stood up.

"Come on, Dad, you're a slacker," said William.

"I just want to pop over to visit Grace," said Harry.

"Can I come?" Harry looked at the eager little face and couldn't imagine not having him around. He couldn't bear to lose him now that he'd just come to live. This was their last weekend before William moved in completely next Sunday.

"No. I won't be long. You go inside and wash up and we'll have a snack when I get back."

Grace opened the door praying it wasn't Jeremy returned to harangue her again. She couldn't stop the spontaneous smile spreading across her face when she saw Harry. It was right on this spot that he'd kissed her that night. Or she'd kissed him and then he'd kissed her. She remembered the way he'd held her and how much passion she'd felt in his lips and his touch.

Her gaze dropped as she felt her cheeks heating up. He had on shorts. His legs were tanned with dirty knees and bits of grass clinging to his socks as if he'd been kneeling in the garden. Grace looked up again, flustered by the almost uncontrollable urge she had to wrap her arms around his neck. One arm anyway.

"I saw that lawyer friend of yours leaving just now," said Harry tersely.

"Did you?" said Grace, astonished by the intense dislike in his voice. Was he jealous of Jeremy coming to see her? Was that possible?

"He filled me in on your plans."

"What plans?" Her face must have given her away as the realization of what he was telling her sank in.

"Do you realize what that will do to me?" demanded Harry.

"To you?" asked Grace keeping her voice level as

guilt fuelled anger billowed up inside at his accusatory tone. "What about this?" She raised her pink cast in front of his face. "What about me? If I can't work? How do I pay the bills then? How do I eat? Where will I live?"

"If you sue me, Grace, I'll have to sell my house and then I won't be able to have William live with me. He'll have to live with his mother and she's moving overseas next year. But I guess you don't care about any of that!"

"I won't sue you, Harry!" yelled Grace. "I never intended to sue you and I'm amazed that you even imagined I would do such a thing."

"Can I believe that, Grace? I never know from one minute to the next what you're going to do and I don't think you do either! How can I possibly believe you?"

"You don't believe anything I say so I don't know. But it's true."

Harry stared at her, his face set and angry. Grace glared at him then grabbed the door and slammed it shut in his face. She stood in the hallway again with her fists clenched. Harry was being totally and utterly unreasonable. Too unfair. How could he think that of her? She'd dismissed suing out of hand as soon as Jeremy mentioned it.

"What was that all about?" asked Eric appearing in the kitchen doorway. "Was that Harry you were yelling at?"

"Yes. He thinks I'm going to go ahead with Jeremy's plans."

"You didn't tell him that nasty idea, did you?" asked Eric in an accusatory voice sounding just like Harry.

"Of course not! Jeremy did. On his way out. They've never liked each other. Now they both hate me."

"For heavens sake go and see Harry and fix it."

"No! He should apologize to me. I've done enough apologizing for things that aren't my fault." Grace stuck her chin up defiantly.

"So you're just going to leave it like that?"

"No," said Grace. "I'm going to call Jeremy and give him the biggest blast he's ever had in his life."

And she marched to the telephone and did just that, ignoring his spluttering and indignation and hanging up a few minutes later with a satisfied expression. New Grace rides again.

Eric, who had been leaning against the door frame listening, applauded.

"Well done, Grace," he cried. "Guess he won't be around any more."

"No." The smile fell from her face and she collapsed into an armchair. Isn't that exactly what she'd had in mind way back when in that discussion with Kirsty? Win Jeremy back and then ditch him? She felt sick in the stomach. Was revenge always such a hollow victory?

"What? You don't care about him, do you?"

"No," she said. "But Eric, Harry won't be around any more either."

"I'll go and sort him out," offered Eric, flopping onto the couch opposite.

"No, no, no," cried Grace. "I have to do it. Just . . . I need to think about it. I have to get Harry to see that I'm not what he thinks I am."

"What does he think you are?"

"An uptight, hard, ambitious ice queen. And that's just for starters. He also thinks I'm flaky and irrational and fickle and can't be trusted from one minute to the next."

"Wow!"

"But he thinks I'm sexy and attractive."

"You are," said Eric. "You should work on that aspect."

"How do you mean?"

"Guys can't resist sexy women."

"This one can and anyway I don't want to just seduce Harry. I want . . ."

Eric raised an eyebrow as she paused. "You want . . . ?" He gestured for her to continue.

"I love him, Eric. I want him to love me." Grace watched Eric's face as she made this admission. They'd known each other for a long time, had dated briefly in their teens but the brief exploratory passion had evolved into the lasting friendship of now. They rarely pried into each other's love lives but Grace knew, of all people, Eric would listen and care.

Eric pondered the news. "Thought so," he said. "I wouldn't be surprised if he already does love you."

"He's good at hiding it," said Grace miserably although her heart lightened a little at Eric's casual assumption.

"Harry's just been through a divorce, he's hardly

likely to hook himself up again without a lot of thought. Plus he's got William to consider."

"Do you do relationship counselling as a sideline?" asked Grace and ducked as a cushion hurtled towards her from the couch.

"Just be normal, Grace. We all told you that right from the start. Harry won't be able to help himself when he meets the real you."

Grace jumped up and kissed Eric on the cheek. "Thanks."

"I just wish I was as good at sorting out my own women," he said and pulled her onto his lap.

"If you stuck to one at a time you'd be better off," said Grace sternly.

"I don't cheat on anyone. They all know I have many girls in my book," he said.

"That's why you're girl-less at the moment, is it?"

"You needn't talk," said Eric indignantly and pushed her off his knee.

Grace barely saw Harry during the next two weeks. They went separately to the last two Italian lessons and eyed each other cautiously from opposite ends of the table, muttering civilities when necessary and neither went to the end of course get together Roberto organized. She reverted to her Old Grace clothes apart from the tight fitting tops which she rather liked.

Marcel and Kirsty phoned to say they wouldn't be

back until close to Christmas because the band had been offered a month of gigs at a holiday resort on the coast.

The weather got progressively hotter. Grace's arm itched and sweated inside the restricting plaster and it was with great excitement and anticipation that she at last went with Eric to have the cast removed.

The doctor took another x-ray promising to give her the results as soon as possible. On the way home in Eric's car she flexed her wrist and wiggled her fingers, marvelling at the lightness and freedom which she'd previously taken for granted. She had an appointment with a physical therapist in the morning where her future would be assessed.

"It feels fine," Grace said to Eric. "I can't wait to try playing."

"Don't overdo it. You have to strengthen it again."

Harry heard the sound of the violin. His hands paused over the keyboard and he listened intently. A smile gradually spread across his face as the playing gathered strength and confidence and Grace launched into the opening bars of the Sibelius concerto she'd been practicing for her audition.

Woof, outside in the back garden, began to howl. Harry jumped up and ran to the back door to stop him before Grace came charging over to complain. He dragged Woof across the lawn by the collar and shoved him into the house. The violin soared on, oblivious.

"You mustn't upset her," said Harry sternly. "You've caused more than enough trouble already." Woof wagged his tail and licked Harry's hand.

The phone rang. Anna said, "Hold onto your hat Harry, I've had a call from a producer in Los Angeles. He wants to buy the film rights to *Time Line*."

Harry sat down abruptly. Woof rested his head on his knee and Harry absentmindedly fondled his ears as he listened to her excited babble. He cut in when something she said registered more clearly than the rest.

"I have to go to LA?" he asked. "When?"

"They'd like you there next week."

"For how long?"

"A week at the most. I'll come with you."

"Yes, please," said Harry fervently. "But what about William? He's moved in with me, Janis has gone to Melbourne and he can't stay with her. It's the end of school and he's got all sorts of things happening here."

"Harry, Harry! Calm down! He can stay with someone."

Harry took a deep breath. "They'll have to take Woof, too," he said.

"Ask around. I'll fix up the dates and flights and call you back," Anna said, all business. "Passport up to date?"

"Yes." Harry hung up and looked at his watch. Nearly time to pick up William. He'd be terrifically excited about the news. It was pretty exciting now that he thought about it. He should tell Grace. She'd be pleased just like she was pleased to hear about William moving in. Harry pushed Woof out of the way, strode to the front door and was half way down the path before he realized what he was doing.

He halted and stood still, feeling like all sorts of an idiot. The violin stopped suddenly, started again. Harry snapped a dead head off a rose bush, listening to the passionate, sobbing sound. He didn't recognize the piece but it was beautiful, very romantic. He lingered and pretended to fiddle with the roses. What had gone wrong between Grace and him? He suspected it was mainly his fault for being judgemental and harsh and comparing her all the time to Janis. She was so beautiful it hurt and those kisses they'd shared had promised delights far beyond anything he could imagine.

Maybe he should . . .

Grace's front door opened and she rushed down the path and stopped. She called out, "I can play, Harry!" And her voice was happy and pleased and excited.

"I heard," he said and smiled. "So did Woof. Did you hear him?" He walked along the footpath and met Grace at her gate. She looked radiantly happy, bursting with pleasure.

"No. I'll be fine, I think. I'm just a bit rusty after six weeks. I'm seeing a physical therapist tomorrow but it doesn't hurt at all."

"Good. Send me the bill."

Her face fell and the light died in her eyes. "That's not what I . . ." Grace turned and walked back towards her door.

"Grace," he called after her. "Grace." She stopped but didn't turn around. "I'm going to America next week. Someone wants to make my book into a movie."

She turned around then and smiled but not with the delight of before.

"Good news for both of us," she said. "Congratulations."

Harry stood wondering if he should grab her and kiss her right then and there the way he wanted to but something made him glance at his watch instead.

"Heavens! William. I have to go."

He raced back to the house to close up and grab his keys. The violin soared out into the quiet afternoon as he jumped into the car and slammed the door. He just didn't seem to be able to get it right with her.

"Who could you stay with, do you think?" Harry asked William as they drove home. "They'd have to take Woof as well."

"Adrian's sister has chicken pox so I can't go there. James has cats, so Woof can't go there." He wrinkled up his face. "I hate the food at Damien's. I'd die if I had to eat it for a week. Yuk!"

"What about that kid who had the party?"

"Jordan. I can't stand him."

"There must be someone," said Harry in exasperation.

"Grace. I can stay with Grace and Eric and then Woof can stay at home." William sat back against the seat with a very pleased expression. “You’ll miss the Christmas concert.”

“I know. I’m sorry.”

“Doesn’t matter. It’ll be terrible. Really boring. Grace can come with me, she won’t mind.”

Harry laughed despite the shock William’s glib assumption had sent coursing through his body.

“And what makes you think Grace and Eric will be happy to have you stay?” he asked. “We don’t know them that well.”

“I do,” said William. “I’ll be on holidays so Grace won’t even have to get me from school.”

Harry shook his head. “We can’t ask them,” he said firmly.

“Why?”

“It’s too much. We just can’t. I’ll think of someone else.”

“I won’t like anyone else,” said William

“Why do you like Grace so much?” asked Harry curiously.

William shrugged. “She’s nice. Will you ask, Dad? Please?”

So Harry had to say yes.

He went over after dinner leaving an impatient William watching TV, and having promised to be his most persuasive. Eric answered the door for which Harry offered up a silent prayer. At least he’d got that far, a foot in the door.

"Come in, Harry," cried Eric. "Congratulations, Grace told me about the movie."

"Thanks," said Harry. So she'd told Eric. That must be a good sign, surely. "But it may not come off. These things can fall through easily."

"But you get a free trip to the States out of it." Eric lead the way to the living room. Grace was sitting on the couch and looked up as they came in.

"Hello." She put the book she was reading down beside her. His book. Harry stared at the familiar cover then met Grace's eye. She smiled. "It's Marcel's." She didn't offer an opinion.

Eric said, "When do you go?"

"They want me there next week. Anna, my agent, has done the bookings and we leave on Wednesday morning."

Harry sat down opposite Grace. She didn't seem interested. Now that she could play again she probably wasn't at all concerned with the goings on of the neighbors. Back on her upward path to the front desks of the orchestra. How to broach the subject . . . William had no idea how difficult this was.

"What about William?" asked Grace suddenly.

"We can watch Woof for you," offered Eric.

Harry glanced at Eric and smiled. "Thanks. I was hoping you might, that's why I came over. He could stay at home and you'd only have to feed him and take him for a walk.'

"And William?" repeated Grace.

Harry took a deep breath. He met Grace's eye firmly. "He wants to stay with you," he said. "He sent me over to ask. I told him I would but I don't expect you to . . ."

"Yes," cut in Grace. "Of course he can come. Eric?"

Eric nodded. "Yup. Fine by me."

"Really?" asked Harry. He smiled as a wave of relief flooded over him. He sank back against the cushions and realized he'd been sitting forward with tension knotting his stomach.

"The only thing is," said Grace. "He'd have to sleep in Marcel's room but Marcel's due back on the Friday. Maybe it would be better if I came over and stayed with him. Less disruptive. Do you have a spare room?"

Harry felt as though he were being left behind as the plan took on a life of its own and Grace started sounding like Janis. Super organizer. Grace in his house? Living there? The thought made his chest tighten. "Not really. It's my study, where I write. But . . ." He paused. "You could sleep in my room."

"Okay, if you don't mind," said Grace without the slightest flicker of emotion. "Is he on holiday yet?"

"Finishes on Thursday but he's got the Christmas concert on Wednesday night." Harry laughed. "He said it would be terrible and boring but that, I quote, 'Grace can take me. She won't mind.' "

Eric gave a guffaw of laughter. Grace smiled and said, "He's right. Eric will take us both."

"Hang on a minute, Grace!" Eric cried.

"You don't have to go, either of you. I'll leave you

the car keys, Grace. I'm really grateful." Harry looked from one to the other and stopped with his gaze firmly on Grace. "I don't know what you've done to my son," he murmured as he stood up. "Bewitched him."

"That's Grace," said Eric cheerfully. "She's irresistible."

"Apparently she is," said Harry. He looked down at Grace who sat calmly on the couch watching him with a slight smile on her face. "Thanks again, Grace. I'm very grateful for this. You've no idea how much."

"See you later, Harry," said Eric and went out quickly.

Grace said, "No *problemo*, Harry. I'm flattered you thought I'd be capable of minding him."

"Like I said, he refused point blank to consider any other suggestions." Harry spread his arms. "What could I do?"

"What indeed?" said Grace drily, "having exhausted all other possibilities."

"Grace, it wasn't like that."

Grace stood up. "No? Would you have asked me?"

Harry sighed. "I wouldn't have been game to after—everything."

Grace stepped closer and Harry's breath came hard in his chest as he smelled her sweet fragrance and his eyes feasted on her lips. She stopped, almost touching his chest and looked up at him with a slight smile playing on her mouth. He could feel the warmth radiating from her body.

"It's much better now without my cast," she said and extended her bare arm to one side to show him. She flexed her fingers. "See?"

The arm hovered in mid-air then moved. Her fingers touched his cheek softly.

"I have to go," he rasped. "William's home alone." Harry turned and made good his escape before all his self control collapsed in a screaming heap.

Harry put the last of his clothes in the suitcase and zipped the lid shut. William sat on the bed and watched.

"Well, that's that!" said Harry. "Are you ready?"

"Yes."

A car horn sounded from outside.

"There's the taxi," shouted William and darted to the front door. Harry heard him open it and when he got to the door lugging his case William was already chatting to the driver.

Harry locked the house and walked down the path. Grace's door opened and she came out to stand on the footpath. She had on a cotton sundress circa nineteen fifty five and looked exactly like a wholesome suburban housewife seeing her husband and child off to work and school respectively. Harry swallowed. He suddenly wished with all his heart she were coming with him. He wanted her to continue where he'd left off the other night. He'd replayed the scene constantly from every possible angle and with all sorts of delicious ways of reaching the inevitable ending.

"Here are the keys," he said gruffly. Grace put them in one of the two square pockets on the skirt of her floral print dress. "House and car."

"Thanks," she said. "Don't worry. I'll pick William up from school this afternoon and we'll go to the concert tonight."

Harry gazed into her gorgeous eyes. He hadn't realized—now it hit home like an avalanche—he didn't want to leave her. Even for a week it seemed too long. "Thanks Grace. I don't . . .' But Grace stepped closer and stretched up to cut off his words and nearly stopped his heart with a soft and gentle kiss.

"Knock 'em dead, Harry," she whispered and he thought he caught the hint of a tear in her eye as she drew away. She leaned forward to wave to William who had already ensconced himself in the backseat of the taxi. "I'll see you this afternoon," she called through the open door.

'Okay. Bye, bye Grace."

The taxi driver swung Harry's case into the trunk and slammed it shut. "Better go, buddy, if we're going to drop the boy at school on the way to the airport."

Harry turned to Grace and gave her a last searching, desperate look trying to memorize her features and imprint her face on his memory. Enough to last seven days. He leaned down and kissed her quickly.

"Take care," he said and then murmured, "I'll miss you," as he turned to get into the taxi.

Grace waved until the car rounded the corner of the

street. Tears ran down her cheeks. Had Harry really said what she thought he'd said? "I'll miss you?" Did he say that? She'd miss him, that was a fact. Seven whole days apart separated by an ocean. They'd never spent that much time without seeing each other since he moved in a few months ago. She'd seen him every week at Italian class and several more times during the week, pottering around the garden or at the shops or walking by with Woof. He was always there, right next door.

In the few days since Harry had come to make his request Grace had hardly been able to think straight. He'd trusted her with his son. His most precious treasure in the world. Not only that, he'd given her the keys to his house and his car. Was he weakening? Could she read a change of attitude? Had he decided she wasn't so crazy after all or was he simply swayed by William's insistence and his own need to find someone to watch him at short notice?

Several things made her lean hopefully towards the former. First up, Harry would have stayed at home rather than leave William with someone he didn't know and trust. She knew he put William first in any decision where his welfare would be affected. Second up, Harry could but never would, have hired someone to watch him, which she knew firsthand several friends of Jeremy's did when they wanted to go on vacation. Extraordinary behavior Grace always thought, privately, when they'd mentioned casually a week in Fiji or skiing at Thredbo without the burden of the children.

No, all the signs were looking favorable for Grace at the moment. She and William would have the best time together and Harry would see once and for all what a reliable, competent, loving woman she could be, that she really was all along.

Chapter Eleven

But Grace and William didn't go to the Christmas concert. Grace had a phone call from the school instead, at lunchtime, saying William was in the nurse's office feeling sick. Could she possibly pick him up? Of course, she could.

She walked with the pale faced, miserable little boy to the car and helped him buckle up. He closed his eyes, slumped against the window. Grace looked across at him anxiously. Chicken pox, the school secretary had mentioned. It's that time of the year and they'd already had several cases notified. Had she had it? Yes, Grace remembered it clearly. Red spots, unbearable itching, scabs—hideous!

"Call the doctor to make certain," suggested the

woman, "but there's not a lot you can do. It could be just a twenty four hour bug, of course."

At home William went straight to his room and sprawled on the bed. Grace followed him in. She pulled off his shoes and socks.

"Want to put on your pajamas and hop in properly?"

He nodded and sat up so that she could undo his shirt. She scanned his chest as he struggled into his pajama top. No sign of any spots yet.

"I'll do the bottom," he said. Grace nodded and went out.

"Like to call your mom?" she asked as she waited outside the door.

"Yes," he said. "But you do it."

"All right. Ready?"

"Yes."

Grace walked over to his bed and pulled the sheet up over him. She placed a hand on his forehead. It was hot and he had a feverish look about the eyes with dark rings bruising the pale, delicate skin.

"I'll get you a cool drink," she said. "Can you take aspirin?"

William nodded. Grace pulled the curtains across to block out the glaring sunlight. She smiled at the anxious face.

"Don't worry. If it's chicken pox it's the best thing to have it when you're a kid. Much worse for grownups. I had it when I was seven. And you don't get it again."

William managed a smile. His eyes closed.

Harry had left several numbers to reach Janis in Melbourne. Grace left two messages then hit the jackpot on the cellular number.

"Does he want me there?" asked Janis when she had absorbed the information. Grace gained the impression it would be very inconvenient. And it wasn't really necessary at the moment, she could cope.

"I'm sure he would but I can manage. I just thought I should let you know," she said.

"Thank you, I appreciate it." Janis sounded as though she were dealing with a business client. "If it is chicken pox, I haven't had it so I should stay away anyway."

"Yes, probably," agreed Grace.

"Keep me informed," said Janis. "And give him my love."

"Do you want to speak to him?" asked Grace quickly before the conversation was ended.

"Tell him I'll call him tonight. Now's a bit—I'll call him. Thanks Grace. I'm sure he's in good hands. Harry would never have left him with you otherwise."

"Should I tell Harry, do you think?" asked Grace ridiculously buoyed by that comment and warming several degrees towards Janis.

"Wait and see how sick he is but I would say no, Harry will only worry and want to rush home which might mess up this opportunity. And it's a big one. He's only away a few days. William will be better by the time he gets back."

"All right," said Grace doubtfully.

"Sorry Grace, gotta go. Thanks for calling. Bye."

Grace hung up and realized she'd forgotten to ask Janis whether William was able to take aspirin. Harry had left a list of numbers for her to call in all sorts of emergencies from the dentist through the fire department to the vet for Woof. She phoned the doctor and was given clear and calm instructions about what to look out for and how to treat her patient.

"Don't worry, it sounds as though he's brewing chicken pox," he finished. "But don't hesitate to bring him to the office if you think you should."

She went back to William with aspirin discovered in the medicine cabinet, a cool drink and a damp cloth to wipe his face. He was asleep, breathing heavily with his mouth partly open and his limbs sprawled over the bed with the sheet twisted around his knees. She straightened it up and gently wiped his flushed cheeks. He stirred and opened his eyes. For a moment she knew he didn't recognize her because he blinked and frowned but she said softly, "It's all right, it's only me, Grace. Can you take this?" She sat on the edge of the bed and showed him the aspirin. "The doctor said it would help you feel better. We're lucky your dad had some."

William sat up painfully and opened his mouth. Grace popped the pill in and he swallowed a big slurp of water to wash it down.

"I called your mom and she sends her love," she said. "She'll call tonight to see how you are."

"What about Dad?"

"He'll still be in the air," said Grace. "Somewhere over the Pacific Ocean. He'll call when he gets to America."

William seemed satisfied and lay back with his eyes closed. Grace stood up but he reached out a hand and grabbed her skirt.

"Stay," he said so Grace sat back down and waited quietly until he went to sleep, occasionally patting his cheek and brow with the damp cloth and wondering how she had been so lucky as to gain the trust of this beautiful child.

She called Eric next door and filled him in. He came later to take Woof out for a walk staying to chat briefly to the invalid. Janis called again as promised and William had a lengthy conversation. Grace offered him soup for dinner and settled him for the night before the realization hit home that she would be sleeping in Harry's bed. She hadn't even been into his room, she'd been so preoccupied with William, she'd simply left her overnight bag in the living room.

She pushed the door open tentatively and peered in, switched on the light. He had a single bed she saw with surprise. And the room was quite spartan apart from a large, dark, wooden wardrobe against one wall and a chest of drawers in one corner. A small red patterned Persian rug saved bare feet from landing on the polished wood floorboards, and plain, forest green curtains screened the window. She dragged them across.

She'd only brought essentials but when she opened

the closet to hang her sundress the scent of Harry overwhelmed her. Her knees went weak and a sob caught in her throat as she buried her face in the shirts and jackets, all emanating Harry so that her longing for him became a physical palpable thing and she had to pull away and sit on the bed leaving her dress in a heap on the floor. She pulled on her nightie and crawled into Harry's narrow single bed hoping to feel some sense of him there too but he'd changed the sheets before he left and they smelled of fresh, clean, laundry detergent.

Did the fact that Harry had purchased a single bed underline his intention of not becoming tangled, as he put it, with another woman? Grace wondered about that. It seemed to her that Harry was barricading himself into his single parent status determined not to let himself be hurt again and when she had come along threatening to undermine his good intentions he'd panicked. Had she got under his skin? Grace smiled. She knew she had. Was it deep enough, though? She wanted to be ingrained like a tattoo not a removable irritation like a thorn.

William called out. Grace got up.

The next morning William's fever had lessened thanks to regular cooling through the night and aspirin and they discovered the first of the red spots on his chest and back.

"You've got it," announced Grace.

"Chicken pox?"

"Yup. I'll have to get some calamine lotion for when

you get itchy. I'll send Eric. He can take Woof for a walk at the same time."

"Mom said we shouldn't tell Dad," said William. "Because he'll worry."

"What do you think?" asked Grace. This was Birmingham family politics and she should abide by the majority decision, she'd decided. She also agreed with Janis's summation.

He screwed up his face. "He'll be back on Tuesday. Will I still have spots?"

"Probably. Scabs definitely and maybe spots still."

"We won't tell him. It'll be a surprise."

"It certainly will," murmured Grace.

Harry called that morning.

"Hello, Grace?"

"Harry, hello. How are you?" she cried and her heart leapt at the sound of his voice albeit he sounded tired and distant.

"Fine, jetlagged. I've been up for days, I think. I'm supposed to be lunching with some hot shot soon. We're waiting to be picked up. What about you? How's William?"

"We're getting on just fine. Don't worry about us. I'll put William on."

"Grace? I . . ."

His voice changed and she barely whispered as her heart now began to pound like a bass drum, "Yes?"

"I . . . I want . . . Grace?" he asked. "Are you still there?"

"Yes," she said her throat tight with anticipation of what he might want.

"Is that Dad?" called William from his bedroom.

"William wants to talk," she said quickly and headed for his room with the phone glued to her ear.

"I'll call tomorrow," said Harry in a totally different voice.

"Goodbye. Here's William." Grace handed the receiver to William who launched into a barrage of questions about Los Angeles which would hardly give Harry a chance to answer let alone ask questions of his own.

Harry sat on the plane home in a fever of anticipation. Anna, content with the success of the venture, slept beside him most of the way. He sat with his eyes closed and his head filled with Grace. She'd been with him the whole time they'd been away and he'd abandoned himself to her with an overwhelming sense of relief and release. All through the talks and lunches and endless negotiating and introductions she'd been by his side, in his head, filling his soul with her smile and her voice and her loveliness.

Their phone conversations had been necessarily but frustratingly brief and focused around William and he had no doubt she'd cared well for his son. They both sounded happy and he imagined, hopefully, she had waited as eagerly for the contact as he had. But he couldn't tell her over the phone how he felt. He wanted to hold her in his arms and tell her how he loved her to her face. And he prayed she still felt the same.

And the hours weren't passing fast enough and the plane wasn't flying fast enough and he couldn't wait to see her.

Harry got out of the taxi and looked at the house in the early morning light. They must be sleeping in. He'd told them not to meet him as it was far too early and inconvenient to ride out to the airport when he could catch a taxi. Grace had agreed very readily which left him with a tinge of disappointment. Perhaps she wasn't as keen to see him as he was to see her after all. Maybe he'd left it far too late, messed her around too much. Maybe her love had died or wasn't the real thing at all, the way he'd so glibly accused her. Still, he'd looked around hopefully for them as he left customs but no sign.

He unlocked the door and walked in. Would Grace be asleep still? In his bed? That thought made his breath catch in his throat.

She wasn't. She appeared in the kitchen doorway and she was wearing the short pink robe she'd had on when he first saw her in the garden. Her legs were bare and beautiful and she gave an inarticulate noise between a sob and a cry. Harry dropped his suitcase. He took a step towards her and stopped, suddenly unsure.

"Hello Grace," he said in a voice hoarse from tiredness and emotion. "I missed you something chronic."

She stared at him. Her lips parted in a smile and all at once Harry knew she felt exactly the same as he did. He held out his arms and she was there, warm and soft and infinitely desirable. Her face lifted to his and her eyes swam with tears, or they might have been his own as his lips met hers gently.

"Dad!" William's cry made him turn sharply and search eagerly for that other face he'd missed so much. But what he saw made him gasp in shock. "I've got chicken pox," announced William and sounded almost proud as he stood in his bedroom door with red spots covering his face and neck and those parts of his hands and feet sticking out from his pajamas.

"Good grief, William!" cried Harry. He released his grip on Grace and strode across to his son. "What? When? How did you?" He turned to her, a chill suffusing his body. "Why didn't you tell me?"

"You'd only worry, Dad. We decided not to," said William. "I'm getting better now."

"Better?"

"Have you had it?" asked Grace quietly. She retied her belt, crossed her arms over her chest.

"What? No, yes. I don't know. Yes," said Harry unable to comprehend what was happening, the deception enacted upon him. By Grace whom he'd trusted, with his son and with his love.

"I'm going back to bed," said William.

"I'll get the bath ready," said Grace.

"All right." William disappeared into his room.

Harry looked at Grace. "I'll get his bath ready," he said. "I'm home now and I'd like to take care of my son, thank you."

Grace regarded him steadily and Harry returned her gaze just as firmly. He ran a tired hand across his face. Grace said, "Would you like some breakfast?"

"No, thanks. I have to see to William. Just tell me Grace, when did he get this chicken pox? How long has he been sick?"

"The day you left," she replied quietly. "I called Janis straight away."

"You called Janis but you didn't bother telling me?" he cried. "All those times we spoke?"

"What could you do, Harry?" demanded Grace. Her eyes glittered with a dangerous light. One he recognized from countless arguments with Janis. "What would you have done?"

"I would have come home," he said.

"Exactly! And done what? I was here. I was coping. Janis spoke to him every day."

"He's my son!"

"And I looked after him for you. Perfectly well."

He exhaled—a long drawn-out rush of air which contained all his frustration, tiredness, disappointment, confusion. His shoulders sagged. "I know. I know. I can see that. Of course, you did. Thank you. But it's just . . . you should have told me he was ill."

Harry strode into William's room, furious with himself and the whole stupid situation. She was so lovely and he thought he loved her and she loved him and for a moment it was wondrously perfect and then she went and deceived him like this. How could she do that? Hopeless! The whole thing was hopeless. He was fooling himself.

"Dad did you get me something from LA?" asked William as Harry closed the bedroom door. "Are they making a movie from *Time Line?* What's it like there? Did you go to Disneyland? Did you meet any actors?"

"I do have something for you but I have to unpack first," said Harry sitting down heavily on William's bed.

"Why were you shouting at Grace?" asked William.

"I wasn't."

"Yes, you were." William stared at Harry, his brow furrowed and stern. "Grace looked after me. She even stayed up in the night to keep me company when I couldn't sleep because of the itching. It itches a lot, Dad. I have to have a bath in special stuff that Grace got and it makes it not itch so much. And she made me special food."

"Oh William." Harry groaned and rubbed his hands over his face. Had he made another monstrous mistake? "I can't think straight. I'm tired. I still feel as though I'm sitting on that plane."

"That's jetlag," said William. "Can you ask Grace if the bath's ready for me?"

"I'll do it," said Harry.

"Make sure you get the temperature right. Grace

knows exactly. Ask her how much of that stuff to put in," said William.

Harry stood up. "I think I have to apologize to Grace," he said.

"You'd better have a shower and shave first," suggested William, "if you want to kiss her again."

Harry grinned and opened the door ready to make yet another apology, plead shock and a temporary mental aberration brought about by fifteen hours in an airplane, and beg forgiveness but when he went to the empty kitchen and then very hastily to his room he discovered she'd gone. He turned the taps on in the bath for William, took his suitcase to his room and sat on the bed mournfully to unlace first one shoe and then the other.

The room had a subtle fragrance—Grace. The bed was still rumpled from her sleeping in it. She hadn't had time to change the linen before he chastised her and abused her, that's of course straight after he'd kissed her and told her he missed her. Who was the crazy, fickle one here? It seemed less and less like Grace and more and more like Harry.

He doubted now whether she'd welcome more apologies from him. He wished with all his heart they could start again. Wipe the slate clean and start completely afresh. And get it right.

Grace grabbed her overnight bag, stuffed her belongings into it while Harry was closeted with William with the door shut against her, and ran. Eric and Marcel were still asleep. They wouldn't be up for hours. Plenty of time to compose herself and prepare a face to present to them.

That was definitely the end of the Harry and Grace story. There was nowhere for it to go from here except around in circles. She'd had enough of that. She'd had enough of men in all their shapes and forms. More than enough. If any man wanted her he'd have to come and get her and take her as she was. Old Grace had gone, New Grace had floundered there was just Grace left, stronger and much, much wiser. A Grace who couldn't even cry any more.

The way of the Tao. According to Myra her destiny cannot be altered and who was she to try meddling with the cosmic forces?

Two hours later Grace sat drinking tea in the kitchen, dry-eyed, drained. She should do some practice. She hadn't touched her violin at all the previous week. She'd be back in the orchestra after the Christmas break, sitting next to Edward again because Vinnie had moved into the coveted second desk position. Somehow she couldn't summon the energy to get herself off the chair and into the living room.

She wondered how William was doing, if Harry had managed to get the bath water the right temperature. And what would he feed him tonight? She'd planned dinner for the three of them, as she imagined Harry would be too jetlagged and out of synch to cope with meals. And what would they do for Christmas? It was only three days away. How had he got on with the movie people?

No! No more wondering about Harry.

Someone knocked firmly on the door. Grace went to answer it listlessly. Harry stood on the step. Her breathing stopped and started and she clutched the door frame because suddenly her legs lost their strength. Harry had showered and changed and he looked very determined and very handsome and unbearably desirable. And all her resolutions blew away on the warm summer breeze which gallivanted down Curston Road. He smiled and held out a single red rose.

"Hello," he said. "I'm your new neighbor. My name's Harry Birmingham. And I would love to get to know you."

Grace tried to smile but failed, instead her whole expression crumpled and all the dammed up tears sprang to her eyes in a flood. She put both hands over her face and only resisted feebly when Harry gently pulled them away and said brokenly into her hair as he wrapped his arms around her, "And I love you."

Grace sniffed hard and said into his shoulder, "My name's Grace Richmond and I love you, too."

Harry drew back and held her face between his hands. He wiped her cheeks with his thumbs. Just before he kissed her he said, "I have a son named William and a dog named Woof."

"I love them too," said Grace when she could speak. "I play the violin."

"I love the violin," murmured Harry and Grace giggled through the next kiss, "You do not."

"I write science fiction," murmured Harry after the next kiss.

"I love science fiction," said Grace and this time Harry laughed and said, "You do not. Come and meet my son."

He pulled the door closed and put his arm around her shoulders. She slid her arm around his waist. Harry bent to pick up the rose which had fallen at their feet. Grace took it and held it to her nose. She stretched up to kiss his cheek but he turned his head and she kissed his mouth instead. Eventually they continued down the path.

"I want to start again, Grace," he said as they swung onto the footpath and headed for his house.

"But I've only just met you, Harry," said Grace. She stopped to sniff the roses lining his front path. "I can't wait to meet your son and your dog."

"Woof loves the violin. He sings," said Harry.

"Oh good." Grace laughed. "I'm sure we'll all get on wonderfully well."

Harry laughed too. "*Certo*," he said.

"I learned Italian," said Grace. "We've got lots in common, haven't we?" She placed her hands on his shoulders and gazed into his eyes.

"Oh yes," he said softly. "And I bet there's lots more we haven't discovered yet."

00411 2838